The Best of Spicy MYSTERY

Volume 1

The Best of Spicy Mystery

Volume 1

BY

JOHN BARD
ROBERT LESLIE BELLEM
JUSTIN CASE
HARLEY L. COURT
HENRY KUTTNER
MORT LANSING
LEW MERRILL
REX NORMAN
COLBY QUINN
JEROME SEVERS PERRY

EDITED BY

ALFRED JAN

BOSTON
ALTUS PRESS
2012

© 2012 Altus Press • First Edition—2012

EDITED AND DESIGNED BY
Matthew Moring

PUBLISHING HISTORY
"Spicy Mysteries Re-Examined" Copyright © 2012 Alfred Jan.
"Hell's Archangel" originally appeared in the April, 1938 issue of *Spicy Mystery Stories*.
"Fiend's Feast" originally appeared in the June, 1938 issue of *Spicy Mystery Stories*.
"Lorelei of Lynnwold Light" originally appeared in the September, 1935 issue of *Spicy Mystery Stories*.
"Murder From Nowhere" originally appeared in the November, 1935 issue of *Spicy Mystery Stories*.
"The Second Mummy" originally appeared in the May, 1936 issue of *Spicy Mystery Stories*.
"Mistress of Vengeance" originally appeared in the August, 1936 issue of *Spicy Mystery Stories*.
"Green Eyes" originally appeared in the May, 1936 issue of *Spicy Mystery Stories*.
"The Head of Mike Vasco" originally appeared in the November, 1935 issue of *Spicy Mystery Stories*.
"Bat Man" originally appeared in the February, 1936 issue of *Spicy Mystery Stories*.
"Mirror Magic" originally appeared in the April, 1938 issue of *Spicy Mystery Stories*.
"Dance of Damballa" originally appeared in the September, 1937 issue of *Spicy Mystery Stories*.

THANKS TO
Alfred Jan & Rick Ollerman

TABLE OF CONTENTS

ALFRED JAN

Of the four titles in Culture Publication's spicy stable, *Spicy Mystery Stories* is the most unique and notorious. The first newsstand copy, dated June 1935, appeared third in the roster after *Spicy Adventure Stories,* November 1934, and *Spicy Detective Stories,* April 1934. *Spicy Western Stories,* November 1936, seemed to be an afterthought.

Spicy Mystery Stories stands out because the three men in charge, Lawrence Cadman, editor, Frank Armer, editor-in-chief, and publisher Harry Donenfeld, individually or collectively, exempted it from the boxed star treatment. During 1936 and 1937, all the other Spicys came out in unexpurgated and expurgated versions whose interior illustrations of women's bodies revealed less flesh, supported by textual changes reflecting this difference. A boxed star placed on the front cover's upper right hand corner signified this censorship, leaving identical front cover paintings. The only nod to image taming in *Spicy Mystery Stories,* oddly enough, does occurs on front covers: the woman in underwear on the June 1935 cover reappears in a dress on the June 1939 cover. Otherwise, graphic descriptions of female bodies coupled with salacious illustrations jump off the page in full force to stimulate male sexual fantasies, hence the notoriety. This clean and sexy strategy was unique among pulp magazine publishers. For a more complete discussion of Culture-Trojan self-censorship, see my essay in *Windy City Pulp Stories* #9, 2009, Black Dog Books, the best compilation of articles on the Spicy pulps to date.

I conceived this project to highlight worthy stories which rise above the warmed over weird menace category found in pulps like *Horror Stories, Terror Tales, Dime Mystery, Uncanny Tales, Thrilling Mystery,* and others. Containing the most formulaic of pulp story plots, they consist of a villain, usually a mad scientist, unscrupulous physician, greedy trust fund manager or land owner trying to achieve nefarious ends by scaring individuals or populations with seemingly supernatural phenomena which turn out in the end not to be; it was just Uncle Charley in a rubber monster suit and phosphorescent paint. After the villain is defeated and exposed by the hero, who always gets knocked unconscious by mid-plot, he and his female companion ride off in the daylight. Endings are always happy. Unfortunately, much of the content in *Spicy Mystery Stories* also fits this description.

On the other hand, this anthology is different. A major theme concerns consequences of overzealous American archeologists who knowingly or unknowingly violate sacred artefacts or people of Third World cultures. Viewed another way, what happens when spicy adventurers come home? Another story shows what can happen when a man falls too hard for a seductive woman. I included a locked-room murder mystery, an unusual find in this title. Henry Kuttner, the famous science fiction author, contributes a semi-weird menace tale to show his thematic breadth. Hugh B. Cave (Justin Case) writes about avenging past wrongs, with a twist ending, and as far as I know, this story has never been reprinted.

Malibu Graphics published the last *Spicy Mystery Stories* anthology in 1990, so it is time to take another look. Most pulp fans collect it for the covers and their rarity, but not for the stories. However, I believe more gems can be found between its covers, and if this volume generates sufficient interest, I anticipate bringing more to light for contemporary readers to enjoy.

A practicing optometrist, Alfred Jan has edited short fiction collections by D.L. Champion (with Bill Blackbeard), Robert Leslie Bellem, and Joel Townsley Rogers, and contributed articles on Norbert Davis, Cornell Woolrich, and other pulp related topics to Blood 'N' Thunder *magazine. Alfred holds an M.A. in Philosophy, specializing in Aesthet-*

ics, and published freelance art criticism from 1982 to 1995. Work in progress includes a sample of works on ethics and aesthetics by the bohemian Gelett Burgess.

ΠELL'S ΔRCΠΔΠGEL

*With Marie at his side, Bob had to be cautious,
though the whole thing was mumbo-jumbo
to him. The very idea that Gilles de Rais,
devil-worshiper and child-murderer, could
be reincarnated in this day and age!*

"**Well we're almost** there," Marie said, brushing a tendril of dark hair from her eyes. "Too bad the car broke down, but we're lucky it was only a few miles from Uncle John's place."

"Blame it on the axle," Robert Gordon, her fiancé, told her flippantly. A few feet away the trail wound off among tall pines, but in the little glade where they sat resting in the late afternoon sun, it seemed as if they were a thousand miles from civilization. "Blame it on the axle, Marie. It doesn't matter, anyway. You've got me along to do the dirty work."

The girl's face was worried. "It's funny, Bob—ever since we left the car I've had a feeling—something strange. I don't know why. There's—"

Gordon put his arm around her waist. "Would a kiss help you forget it?"

As always, he thrilled to the ecstasy of her lips, the perfumed warmth of her breath. Her hand caressed his cheek gently.

"Still feel strange!" he asked at last.

She smiled a little, and then sobered. "It's my imagination, I suppose. But I *do* feel worried, somehow. As though there's a blanket hanging over these mountains—like a sheet of glass. Something you can't see, but that you can sense."

"Getting morbid on me!" Gordon chuckled. His arms tightened about her slim body, drawing her closer. He could feel her pliant breasts cushion against his chest, and a flood of emotion swept him. She was wearing little besides a khaki shirt and shorts. He could feel her warmth, the supple muscles of her back through the thin shirt as his hand slid up to her shoulder, to the nape of her neck, then cupped the back of her head while he kissed her.

"Bob…" she murmured. Her eyes were luminous. She twisted suddenly, lay back against his chest, her shirt temptingly opened at the throat. He bent, pressing his lips to the smooth whiteness where neck melted into shoulder. The shorts crept up unnoticed, baring the tanned flesh of her thighs. Her breath was fluttering

Together he lifted cross and girl and flung them into the flaming pyre!

in his ear....

She straightened abruptly, her mouth open in a square of fear.

"Bob!" She was staring past him—and Gordon turned his head, followed the direction of her eyes. He sprang to his feet. Instinctively, he pulled Marie up with him, held her close at his side.

A man was standing a short distance away, and in one hairy hand he held a cross crudely constructed of branches. Something was crucified upon it—something red and bleeding and utterly horrible, mercifully dead. A small animal—perhaps a rabbit.

For the first time Gordon saw Hell's Archangel.

His face was very dark, very bony, with gaping hollows in the cheeks and temples. The eyes were almost invisible, sunk in their sockets and overshadowed by shaggy eyebrows. The man had a mop of thick, dark hair and wore an ordinary lumberjack's outfit. In his hand was a knife.

Its blade was stained with crimson, and shreds of dark fur clung to it. Gordon watched the blade, alarmed yet unaccountably fascinated. But the man made no hostile move, though his eyes seemed to gloat on the rounded whiteness of Marie's breast, half revealed by the partly-open shirt.

"What are you doing here?" Gordon rapped out curtly.

The other drew himself erect, his eyes blazing from their cavernous sockets. It was as if a mantle had fallen suddenly on the bony shoulders, giving the man an air of fantastic majesty. His voice boomed out, resonant and deep.

"You question *me?* You—dare?"

Gordon moved slightly so that his body shielded Marie. That knife....

"Sure," he said. "And why not? Who are you?"

For a long moment the man glared. Then his voice, organ-deep, roared out.

"I am Gilles de Rais!"

Gordon felt a chill crawl down his spine. Gilles de Rais—devil-worshipper and child-murderer, who had been condemned and executed by the Inquisition in 1440! That infamous name was familiar to Gordon. Gilles de Rais, he knew, had been the most notorious sadist of medieval times! Frowning he eyed the gaunt face of this man who carried a cross with its ghastly burden. He said slowly:

"Well—that's your business. Can you tell me if I'm on the right trail to the Meagher hunting lodge?" The man was insane, Gordon realized. And, with Marie at his side, he couldn't afford to take chances. It was safer to humor him. But "Gilles de Rais" was not so easily placated.

The horribly lean face was grim. "You doubt me?" he roared. "You doubt that the soul of Gilles de Rais, freed by the flames of the Inquisition's funeral pyre, has returned to earth in this body, by the grace of *Astaroth et Asmodée*. You fools!"

Gordon moved forward, but Gilles stepped into his path, the blood-stained knife raised threateningly. "Fools, I said!" the devil-worshipper thundered. "You should be blinded by the sight of my face! I have been honored above all men; even the Master has revealed himself to me. I saw him—"

Gordon heard Marie catch her breath in a little gasp of fear. But he dared not move his eyes from the contorted face of Gilles. The man propped his cross against a tree, and his voice dropped to a low, almost confidential rumble.

"I saw Him, I tell you. He came robed in crimson, shining with the flames of Hell, and I fell down and worshiped him. Here in the forest, by the altar I made. He whispered that I had served Him well—and He made me an archangel! Look here!"

Gilles ripped at his shirt, baring his chest. On the skin was an inflamed patch of discoloration, shaped like a crude crescent.

"D'you see that? *His* mark—the Sign of the Horns! Fools, you should bow down and worship me!"

Gordon felt his anger rising. If he had been alone he would have attempted to force his way past this mad blasphemer. As it was, he merely said quietly, "Yes, I know. Let us pass, won't you?"

Gilles stepped back, chuckling. His thick thumb caressed the crimson blade of the knife. He gestured widely.

"Oh, pass, pass on, my friends. Go with my blessing. But first—" The sunken eyes were mocking. "First you must bow at the cross. You must pay your respects to the Master."

"I'll be damned if I will!" Gordon snapped, anger overcoming his caution. "Get out of the way, you driveling halfwit, or I'll smash that ugly face of yours so it won't be so blinding. By God—"

"*Stop!*"

Gordon paused at the menace in the man's sudden bellow. He stepped back warily.

"You speak that name here—you dare—!" Gilles' face was blacker than ever. He seemed choking with rage. Then, with an inarticulate snarl, he raised the knife and plunged at Gordon.

Marie saved Gordon's life. With one quick motion she snatched up a handful of dirt from the ground, flung it over Gordon's shoulder into the killer's face. For a second his attention was diverted. And in that second Gordon acted.

He sprang forward, reaching for Gilles' knife arm. He gripped it just in time, as the knife began its downward plunge. Then the two men locked in murderous struggle.

Gilles was tremendously strong. Great muscles writhed in that deceivingly gaunt body. It took all Gordon's strength to keep the knife from descending. Gilles snarled obscenity into his opponent's face.

God, the man was strong! The knife was coming down, very slowly, but inexorably, straight for Gordon's throat. He could not arrest its motion. It pricked his skin—

The great binding arms relaxed. The heavy jaw dropped, and Gordon staggered back, sick and giddy, as Gilles slumped to the ground.

Marie had a heavy branch in her hand. She cast it away, shuddering. Gordon looked down at the unconscious devil-worshiper.

"You knocked him out," he said, grinning. "Good for you. But—what's the matter!"

Marie was paper-white. She put her hand to her forehead and swayed. Then she fainted.

Gordon caught her as she fell. A pang of fear shot through him as he eyed the girl's face, deathly pale in its frame of disarranged dark hair. She was very dear to him, just then. Hastily he lowered her to the ground, and, kneeling, began to chafe her wrists.

Her eyelids fluttered, lifted. Fear sprang into them, and slim arms went about Gordon's neck, drawing him close. "Bob," she whispered. "I—I'm afraid—"

He gripped her tightly, and she clung to him, her lips seeking his. A flame of ecstasy leaped within him as Gordon felt the softly rounded velvet of her breasts against him. When their lips drew apart the girl was breathless, flushed.

Crunching footsteps brought Gordon to his feet. Peering through the bushes near by, he saw two men approaching along the trail. Involuntarily Gordon's eyes went to the broken branch, but a second glance reassured him. "Mr. Meagher!" he called. "How about some help?"

John Meagher, Marie's uncle, ran into the little clearing to Gordon, a surprised expression clouding his features. He was a middle-aged, thick-set man with a hard, craggy face and a bristle of iron-gray hair. Most of his life had been spent in Alaskan mines, and his general appearance bespoke his hardy background.

"What's the matter, Bob?" he asked quickly. "Is Marie hurt?"

Gordon explained briefly. Meagher nodded, but made no other response except a silent lift of his eyebrows toward the cross and its gruesome burden. Gordon, following his gaze, looked around for the man who had called himself Gilles de Rais. He had vanished! He must have crawled away just as the others came into the clearing. Now, however, Gordon became conscious of the presence of another man—a slim, almost dwarfish figure whose straw-colored hair, protruding front teeth and furtive eyes were unpleasantly reminiscent of a rat. A straggling growth of beard added to the illusion. The man looked at him, and then hastily averted his eyes—a habit of his, Gordon learned later.

"Introduce us, Meagher," the little man suggested. His voice was high-pitched and rasping.

Gordon helped Marie to her feet, and she made an attempt to re-button her shirt.

"The lodge is just around the bend," Meagher said. "Uh—this is Jim Hobson, a friend of mine. He's visiting me at the lodge."

"Glad to meet you." The small man extended a small hand gingerly, and hurriedly extricated it from Gordon's handshake. As they moved along the trail, Meagher said:

"Gilles is an odd fish, all right. But he's harmless. He's a trapper, French-Canadian, but he's never bothered anyone, to my knowledge. But if he's doing knife tricks—"Meagher frowned, whistling between his teeth. "It won't do. I'll have to get in touch with the authorities."

A man and a woman greeted them at the hunting lodge—a comfortably rustic cottage set down in the wilderness. One Gordon knew—Meagher's Japanese man-of-all-work, whose usually stolid face grinned expansively at sight of the party.

"Hi, Tommy," Gordon called. "How's tricks!"

"Okay," said the Japanese.

"He's a man of few words, you know," Meagher chuckled. "I think that's the first thing Tommy's said all day. This—this is Sylvia Dorte."

Meagher hurried into the lodge. Marie and Hobson followed, leaving Gordon with Sylvia Dorte. The woman was surprisingly beautiful. The fullness of her lips in a pale, milky face seemed to belie the slight hardness at the corners. Her hair was red-gold, very long, curling about her shoulders. She wore a black knitted sweater which clung provocatively to ample breasts that trembled and swayed as she stepped forward to meet Gordon. Her eyes were tawny, lazily amused.

She said in a slightly husky voice, "This is a pleasure. I hope you'll stay for a while."

Before Gordon could answer Meagher was beckoning them into the house.

"Bob," he said softly, drawing him aside, "why are you here?"

"Didn't you get our letter?"

A change came over Meagher's face. "You sent a letter?"

"Yes. You always said Marie could spend her vacations with you, and I drove her up. Didn't want her to go through the woods alone. But if it's not—"

A shadow fell across them. Hobson came forward, ruffling his mouse-colored hair. Meagher broke in, interrupting.

"It isn't that, Bob. It's only unexpected, that's all. We'll be rather cramped for room, but if Marie doesn't mind that, she's welcome. You too, if you want."

"Sure," Hobson seconded. "Don't let Sylvia and me put you

As he bent over the altar, hatchet raised, something rose up behind the structure.

out any."

"Thanks," Gordon said, eying the man's thin, rat-like face sharply. His eyebrows drew together.

For Hobson's face seemed covered with blood....

Almost at once Gordon realized that it was an illusion, and, looking over his shoulder, he saw through the window the red ball of the sun sinking beyond the pine-tops. Nevertheless a curious little note of warning throbbed in his brain. The words of the devil-worshiper recurred to him—"He came robed in crimson, shining with the flames of Hell." But why should he think of that now!

Meagher was busy arranging for Marie and Gordon, talking with the Japanese. Presently he took the girl to her room. "You'll want to rest, and brush up a bit! Eh!"

Gordon wandered off among the pines, smoking and wondering....

"Mr. Gordon." He knew that throaty voice. Sylvia Dorte's. The woman came from behind a tree, her heavy-lidded eyes intent on his. "Out for a stroll?"

"Yeah," he said, conscious of the alluring curves beneath the close-clinging black sweater. "I thought I'd—"

"Mind if I come along?" She saw the direction of his glance, and smiled. Companionably she linked her arm with his. A little thrill went through Gordon at the closeness of her body.

Soon they were out of sight of the house. She stopped beside a towering pine, pointed up.

"See that!"

Gordon made out the outline of a platform among the branches. He nodded.

"It's awfully nice up there at sunset—Mr. Gordon." Mockery throbbed in the husky voice. "How about a lift?" She indicated the spikes driven into the tree. Silently Gordon clasped his hands, lowered them until she could place one small foot in the support they made. She drew herself up slowly, and the pressure of one knee was warm against his chest as she leaned to reach the spikes. A strange musky perfume, exotic and compelling, was strong in Gordon's nostrils.

She swung herself up into the branches, with a flash of long legs and a swirl of filmy lace. Her face peered down at him.

"Coming up?"

Gordon's throat was a little dry. He reached up, gripped a branch—and hesitated as something soft and flimsy dropped beside him. The woman's voice whispered, "I think I dropped something. Bring it up—will you?"

He bent, lifted the black sweater, still redolent of the curious perfume. Stuffing it into his pocket, he began to climb, glancing up once to see white flesh pale against the green of pine-needles.

She was waiting on the platform, leaning back with her hands clasped behind her head, conscious of the beauty of her body—flaunting it before him. Her full breasts were barely concealed by a scarlet bandeau. Her skin gleamed pallid in the near darkness. The thin skirt had crept above her bent knees and shadowed the smooth curves of her thighs.

Breathing unevenly, Gordon dropped beside her. Her fingers stole up to caress his face, as his arms drew her supple form closer. Trembling with the intensity of her emotion she drew Gordon's face down to the silken hollow of her throat, her fingers digging into the nape of his neck.

She whispered, "Bob... why did you come here?"

He told her. Yet she did not seem satisfied. She held him away, her eyes probing his. Questioning... almost imploring. "No, Bob—is that the truth? Is it?"

Before he could answer the voice of Hobson came in a shrill call. Sylvia drew back, her eyes widening. Gordon's arms went about her, but she wriggled free.

"No—please, Bob." She slipped away, straightened her skirt over tapering white legs, pulled the black sweater on. She smiled as she turned to the edge of the platform. "We'll meet later..."

He didn't answer. Suddenly Gordon found himself thinking of Marie—her slim, wholesomely tanned body, the way her eyes met his, the way her hand dwelt on his arm in a caress. A little disgusted with himself, he followed Sylvia to the lodge. Dinner was ready.

Though he knew Sylvia was waiting, he ignored her and followed Marie to her room after the meal. She eyed him intently.

"Bob—"

"Yeah?" He was comparing her to Sylvia—and the latter was suffering by the comparison.

"Before dinner—when you went out in the woods—" She broke off suddenly, moved forward, arms extended. "Oh, Bob—it doesn't matter. Only I love you so much—"

Cursing himself, Gordon took Marie in his arms. Through the thin blouse and khaki shirt the fragrant warmth of her body was a madness that made his pulses pound—but a madness that was different, far different, from Sylvia's exotic allure. The shirt slipped aside, baring the upper slopes of velvety, firm breasts.

He buried his lips in the hollow of her throat, feeling the smooth flesh pulsating beneath his touch. The nearness of her was all perfume and all delight. His hands slipped down, about her waist, drew her crushingly close.

"Marie…" His breathing was quick and uneven.

Her lips silenced him. And Gordon forgot all else but the magic ecstasy of a throbbing body that pulsed with ardor against his own….

The moon rose late, a great yellow globe that made the forest almost as light as day. About ten o'clock Sylvia Dorte wandered into the lodge's great living-room. A fire blazed in the stone fireplace, and she eyed the group that sat around it. A smouldering glow burned in her amber eyes. She burst out without preamble.

"I can't find Jim. He's gone. Seen him, Meagher?"

"Why, no." Meagher's craggy face showed surprise. "I haven't seen him for hours. What—?"

Then the screams began.

They ripped out, echoing frightful fear, ear-piercing and shrill. And they came from outside the house—thin with distance, but high-pitched and penetrating. Meagher was on his feet abruptly, plunging toward the door.

Marie was staring at Gordon out of wide, terror-brimming eyes. Sylvia Dorte's red lips were twisted. The little Japanese, his face grayish, came pattering in.

At the door Meagher turned. He gestured to a table near by. "There's a gun in the drawer," he called. "Get it, Marie. Stay here till we get back. Stay with Marie and Sylvia, Tommy."

Then he was gone, Gordon trailing him. And Gordon's face was grim as he raced on, those ghastly screams tingling in his ears. Only stark horror could ever drag such shrieks from any creature's throat....

But Gordon was not prepared for the sight that greeted him when, with Meagher at his side, he burst into a clearing in the forest where a tiny fire flickered wanly in the cold moonlight. The screams came from beyond the fire, where a man lay spread-eagled on the ground, his arms and legs tightly bound to stakes. It was Hobson.

The fear of death was making him scream. For across the clearing a tree was arched, bowed, like a catapult. And from it two ropes led down. One passed above the fire, and this was slowly being burned through. The other was looped about Hobson's neck. The purpose of the diabolical device was evident. When the fire burned completely through the rope, the tree would snap upright....

Hobson turned a contorted face toward them and cried out, a rasp of horror in his voice. With a curse Gordon broke the nightmare spell that had bound him, raced forward.

He was too late.

The fire licked up hungrily. With a loud crack the rope parted. The tree shot upright like a spring suddenly released.

And Hobson's cry was choked off, abruptly. Bed drops spattered Gordon's face.

He jerked to a halt, his stomach churning. Something was rolling and bounding across the clearing... something that came to rest, glaring up with blind eyes....

"*God!*" Meagher's giant hand clamped on Gordon's shoulder. "Good God! D-did you see that! God in Heaven!"

The big man was shaking as though with ague. His lips were sleekly pendulous, his face wet with perspiration.

"That damned Gilles," Gordon said thickly. "He did it. I'm going back to the lodge. We can't help poor Hobson now. And Marie and Sylvia are alone there, except for Tommy."

"Eh!" Meagher's face was almost green. "He wouldn't dare!"

Gordon shrugged, casting a significant glance into the clearing. "Come on. We've got to look out for the others now—and for ourselves."

Gordon was first through the door of the lodge, which stood ajar. He almost stumbled over something which rolled away from his feet. The room was dark, except where the moonlight flooded through the doorway.

"Marie!" he called. "Marie!"

There was no answer. From Meagher's lips came a shocked exclamation. Wordlessly he pointed down.

Following his gesture, Gordon saw a thing that grinned up at him in a ghastly mockery of mirth, and blood smeared it from the black, dank hair to the stub where the neck should have been.

Gordon whispered. "Tommy. Gilles… got him."

The room showed traces of a struggle. The little Japanese had put up a desperate fight before being overcome. There were bullet holes in the wall, but the gun itself was gone. In the fire-place, charred and sending out a sickening stench, was Tommy's headless body.

Gordon could never quite remember what happened after that. He shook off restraining hands, plunged out into the shadows where a mocking moon blazed downward with white radiance. Vaguely he could recall racing insanely between giant pines. The night noises of the woods echoed his voice sardonically. A great cat screamed far away. Startled deer bounded past, their stubby white tails flashing. At first, Gordon thought he heard a voice calling him, but presently this died away and was gone. He was alone in the night.

A measure of sanity returned, and he hesitated. It was very still now. Stars glittered frostily above, and the cold moonlight flooded the open space in which he stood….

But that was not moonlight—not that faint glimmer of scarlet that flickered, far away, among the trees.

Gordon shaded his eyes. But nothing was visible except an evanescent shimmer, red and glowing, in the distance. A tongue of flame licked up. Abruptly a bellow of harsh triumph came.

Good God! What was this nightmare saturnalia of blasphemy and terror into which he had blundered? Icy sweat trickled into

Gordon's eyes as he hurried through the trees toward the distant firelight. The roaring voice grew louder as he progressed. It must be the voice of Gilles.

In a great clearing a tall stake had been erected and around its base fagots were piled. Flames were licking up hungrily from the pyre. Bound to a wooden cross that lay on the ground nearby was the half-naked body of Sylvia Dorte, her red-gold hair in mad disarray about her bare shoulders. She was sobbing, striving to free her outstretched arms.

Above her stood Gilles de Rais, his voice raised in a roaring chant. Abruptly he knelt beside the girl, his huge hands sliding roughly over her white form. She shrieked with terror.

The madman crouched, his fingers pressing bruisingly into Sylvia's soft flesh. Gordon moved forward stealthily—

Then, without warning, sharp teeth seemed to sink into Gordon's leg. Caught unawares, he stumbled and came crashing down. A million fiery sparks seemed to explode inside his head. He stretched out an exploring hand, felt the hot stickiness of blood.

Through a haze of mounting dizziness he tried to drag himself erect, conscious only of the agonized screams that came from the clearing. They ended at last, and just before the dark veil swept down Gordon saw Hell's Archangel lift the cross to which Sylvia's body was bound—lift it with two huge arms and hurl it into the midst of the flaming pyre!

A low chant brought Gordon back to consciousness. Warned by some obscure impulse, he lay quietly for a moment, trying to gather his strength. He turned his head furtively and glanced around. A blood-stained rock near him showed what had happened. Pain still throbbed through his leg. Looking down, he realized that a trap had been set at the edge of the clearing—one of many, no doubt—and he had blundered into it.

The chant sounded more loudly; Gilles de Rais strode about the clearing, foam on his contorted mouth. Luckily for Gordon, he was hidden in a clump of bushes. Horror struck through him at the scene in the clearing.

Only a smouldering pile of coals marked the spot where the

pyre had been. And a blackened bone or two protruding from the embers revealed Sylvia Dorte's fate. Near the center of the clearing was—an altar.

It was crudely constructed of flat stones, piled one upon another and cemented with clay. A motionless form lay on it, one arm hanging laxly. It was Marie. A breath of relief touched Gordon as he noted the steady, slow rise and fall of the arched breasts that pushed tautly against her khaki shirt.

The madman sprang toward the altar, gibberish pouring from his writhing lips. He snarled insane laughter as he bent over the unconscious girl, ripped at her clothing till she lay almost nude on the stone altar. He crouched over her, his lips drawn back in a feral grin.

His eyes gloated on the slim, rounded legs, the lyric curve of her hips, and his hands reached out, touched with rough fingers the creamy white skin of her arms, stroked it. He chuckled with delight—and as soft, firm flesh dented beneath hairy fingers, Gordon thanked God that Marie was unconscious.

And then Gilles paused. From a pouch that swung at his side he drew white ashes, scattered them over the girl. Gordon could guess from where those ashes had come.

In silent desperation he turned to examine the trap that held him prisoner. A short length of chain ended in an iron ring that was spiked immovably into a tree-trunk. Gordon tried to pull the vicious jaws apart, but could not. The spring was too strong.

He dared make no sound. If the devil-worshiper should catch sight of him—he forced his mind from the thought. And, as he glanced around hastily, he saw a thick, broken branch lying not far away.

It was almost beyond his reach. Gordon wriggled forward, stretching his arm until muscles seemed to snap in his shoulder. His fingertips touched the rough bark, and with a little gasp he pulled the branch toward him. A sudden noise from the clearing brought his head around sharply.

Gilles was bending over the altar where Marie lay motionless. And in the man's hand was a gleaming, short-handled hatchet. Little flecks of foam dotted Gilles' lips. Gordon almost cried out in horror. He began to work frantically with the broken branch. If he could pry the jaws of the trap apart—

It was not easy. Gordon knew that he could not free himself in time. Nevertheless he strained against the great spring, gasping curses, darting quick glances into the clearing. And therefore he saw the apparition almost before Gilles did.

As the Satanist bent over the altar, hatchet raised, something stirred and rose up from behind the crude structure—something red that shone with a weird, icy glow in the moonlight. Gilles gave a great cry. The hatchet dropped from his hand as he fell to his knees.

He shouted, "Master! You've returned!"

The creature loomed behind the altar, staring down at Gilles. Cold fire bathed it, flickering over the loose scarlet robe that fell from its shoulders. A leering grin revealed two great fangs sprouting from the cavernous mouth, and two odd, knobby projections were visible on the thing's hairless head. Gilles writhed on the ground in abject worship.

"Master! You have honored my sacrifice....*Asmodée!*"

Eerily came a voice, chill and passionless and distant. There was a curious quality of depth to it, as though it spoke from far underground.

"Gilles de Rais," it said quietly. "You have dared to disobey me."

Gilles ground his face into the dirt. "No—no! A greater sacrifice than you demanded...."

"Silence! I required the life of a man and a woman—two of my enemies. Not the life of this girl! Nor of any others!"

The devil-worshiper muttered, "Those two are dead. I killed them, as you ordered."

The distant voice was icy; the red-robed body a startling contrast to Marie's nude, prostrate body. "Yes. But no more, Gilles. Let the girl go free. I wish no more bloodshed."

Gilles hesitated. He said slowly, "You are the god of blood. When I served you in France, long ago, I slew hundreds for your pleasure, and you said you honored me for that. Why—?"

"Do you question me, Gilles de Rais? Do you—dare?"

"She should die!"

"I do not wish it. Go. Go quickly. And do not return."

Gilles dragged himself upright. His face working, he turned away. He took a few steps across the clearing.

And paused. He stood stock-still. Black murder and madness were in his contorted face. The blood-lust in his shattered brain glared out of sunken, blazing eyes.

He shouted, *"No! She shall die!"*

Roaring, he swung about and sprang toward the altar, his great arms lifted. Something cracked sharply.

Gilles stopped, staring. He looked down at his chest from which blood was suddenly spurting. His jaw dropped.

"Asmodée!" he choked. "You—you—"

The devil-worshiper dropped. He crumpled in a boneless, twisted heap. And he lay motionless before the altar.

Gordon watched, frozen with amazement. The shining red-garbed figure was doing incredible things. It was taking off—

"Meagher!" Gordon shouted. "By Heaven—*Meagher!*" Swiftly he bent, wrenched at the branch, heedless now of noise. The jaws of the trap strained apart. Then Gordon was limping across the clearing. The face of John Meagher, white and startled, peered at him from above the shapeless, billowing robe that glowed with crimson fire.

The two men faced each other behind the altar on which lay the unconscious girl. A hasty glance reassured Gordon; Marie still breathed. He looked up to see Meagher's eyes fixed on him inscrutably. And as he returned the stare a look of dawning, amazed comprehension spread over his own face.

"So you're—Gilles' devil," he said tonelessly. "You're behind all this."

Meagher hesitated. He looked down at the gun in his hand. Finally, as though coming to a decision, he pocketed it beneath the robe and shrugged.

"Yes, Bob. You know, now. I'd hoped you'd never know the truth —neither you nor Marie. But—but what else could I do? You don't know—"

Gordon did not answer. Meagher winced beneath the horror in the younger man's eyes. He said quickly:

"Listen, Bob; I'll tell you the whole thing. Those two—Hobson and Sylvia Dorte—were blackmailing me. They knew me in Alaska, where I'd been in a scrape. A man died in a Juneau saloon—I was drunk at the time, but that's no defense in law. Anyway I escaped, and thought no one know. Then, a few weeks ago, Sylvia and Hobson turned up. They had recognized me from a newspaper photograph, and were determined to bleed me dry as the price of their silence about that Juneau affair."

Meagher's face twitched. "I pretended to give in. And then I remembered—Gilles. He'd always been queer—always thought he was a reincarnation of Gilles de Rais. So I decided to use him as my tool. I had Tommy, on a trip to town, get what I needed, and I made this outfit—with phosphorescent paint, a mask, and some putty. One night when Gilles was worshiping at his altar I stepped out from behind a tree and told him that I was Satan, come to earth to reward his faithfulness. He believed me.

"After that it was easy. I told him I demanded two sacrifices— the man and woman at the lodge. But I swear, Bob, I never thought Marie or you would be involved—or poor Tommy. If I had known you were coming I'd have wired you to stay away."

Gordon said, "We wrote you—"

"Hobson picked up the mail in town. He opened it, I guess. He'd seen pictures of Marie around the house, and perhaps he liked the idea of having her at the lodge. Before I had a chance to speak to you alone he drew me aside and told me to keep quiet—to let Marie stay at the lodge."

"But you got more than you'd bargained for," Gordon said hoarsely. Meagher turned away.

"Yes. If I'd—"

He stopped suddenly. Gordon looked up.

Beyond the altar towered— Gilles! Swaying, his clothing drenched with crimson, his gaunt face that of a devil, he confronted the two men. His writhing lips parted. Blood gushed from them, spattering Marie's white, gently heaving bosom.

He gasped, "You can't—kill me! I am—*Gilles de Rais!*"

In his hand was the hatchet.

"*She—shall die!*" he snarled.

He toppled forward. The murderous blade came plunging down at Marie's throat.

Before Gordon could move Meagher flung himself at the altar. He could not hope to intercept the deadly blow. But he threw his body over Marie's, shielding her.

A roaring shout came from Grilles' throat. He staggered back, his eyes glaring blindly. Blood bubbled thickly past his lips. As he fell, Gordon's eyes went to Meagher.

John Meagher had saved his niece from death—but the blade of Gilles' hatchet had bitten deep into his brain. He had died instantly.

A little moan from Marie spurred Gordon to action. He lifted Meagher's corpse away, took the girl tenderly in his arms. Her eyes fluttered open. She gave a little gasp and clung to him.

"Bob! I—what's happened! That man—Gilles—broke into the house and killed Tommy—and I must have fainted—" Then Marie's glance rested on the bloodstained corpse of Gilles. Her face went white.

Gordon gently let her down on the altar. He hesitated, and then a look of decision came into his eyes. He bent over Meagher's still form, reached inside his coat swiftly. With quick strides he went to the smouldering embers of the fire and dropped several objects into it—a red, weirdly shining robe and a hideous, grinning mask. These he buried beneath glowing coals. That done, he returned to the altar, wincing with the pain in his wounded leg.

As he lifted Marie's slim, white body, his gaze went to the dead face of John Meagher, staring up blindly in the moonlight. Slowly he nodded.

"It's okay," he whispered, almost inaudibly. "She'll never know, Meagher. It's our secret. You've earned that, anyway. Whatever you did—I think you've paid the debt."

ROBERT LESLIE BELLEM

FIEND'S FEAST

No girl—not even the one who had killed herself
over him—had filled him with this peculiar
sense of fascination that Vulpa exerted. He no
longer thought it strange that he was to kill her
husband... the man who couldn't be killed!

***T**he prospect of* murdering Stepan Donnwyczi in cold
blood did not fill Burton with any particular sense of revul-
sion. True, he felt a certain mild surprise when Vulpa, Stepan's
exotic wife, suggested the killing; but he was not shocked.

"If you really love me," Vulpa drawled, "you will do this thing
I ask of you."

It was in Burton's Park Avenue apartment, and oblique rays of
crimson sunset filtered through the Venetian blinds of the living-
room to make a misty, blood-red halo around Vulpa's auburn hair
and to accentuate the carmine of her full, sensuous lips as she
sprawled lazily on the leather divan. "You will kill Stepan if you
really care for me," she repeated slowly.

When he looked at her, Burton's entire being thrummed with
tautly-twanging vibrations of yearning. His throat felt parched,
constricted; his palms were moist with sweat. In the past, there
had been many women in his apartment; but they were all forgotten now. Vulpa's wanton, pagan beauty had erased all his memories of the ones who had been here before....

"You really want me to commit murder?" he asked.

"Yes." She had discarded her tea-frock and slip and donned

*"Once, in Mongolia,
Stepan killed one of his
parents—and ate him!"*

the negligee which he had given her for this occasion—her first visit to his quarters. Like green sea-foam matching her exotic eyes, the gossamer chiffon swirled and fluffed about her seductive contours as she stirred against the cushions.

"Yes. I want you to commit murder."

"But why?"

She smiled, her sharp white teeth flashing against the crimson of her lips. "Because I hate Stepan," she answered. Her voice was thick and rich and purring, with a feline texture that held a slurring hint of Balkan accent. "I have hated him for years. And I want you to prove your love for me."

Burton studied her and ached to crush her in his arms. Her full, unbrassiered breasts were tempting globes of yielding whiteness

through the diaphanous chiffon. They stirred gently with her breathing, and a heavy fragrance drifted from the deep valley between them. No girdle confined the contours of her hips; her bare skin gleamed mistily through the negligee, except where lacy black step-ins made a tantalizing contrast. Snowy were her thighs, where the kimono fell away from satin-smooth flesh; and her legs were tapered perfection that thrilled Burton's senses.

"If I were to kill Stepan, then your love would belong only to me…!" he demanded.

"To you, and to no other man."

He went to her; sat on the edge of the divan beside her. His hands strayed to her shoulders, dislodging the negligee. The tumescent slopes of her bosom were impossibly white, with tiny blue veins making a network under silky skin. His fingers burned feverishly as he touched her.

It was curious, he thought, that she possessed the ability to stir him so deeply. He'd known dozens of women in his time; but none had ever filled him with this peculiar, almost hypnotic sense of fascination. Even the ones who had actually loved him—and one girl had committed suicide when he tired of her—were forgotten now. Vulpa Donnwyczi was in his bloodstream, like an insidious poison. He was drunken with the idea of having her love for "his own, never to share it with another man. The last vestiges of his atrophied conscience were throttled; the idea of becoming a murderer brought him no qualms at all.

"You're sure you mean it?" he asked as he stroked her bare arms.

"I'm positive." She shuddered a little. "If you only knew—"

"If I only knew what?"

"How I hate Stepan... and fear him. How his very presence nauseates me... ugh! That cannibal!"

"Cannibal?" Burton sat up and stared into her green eyes.

Her lips were tremulous. "Perhaps I shouldn't have told you that. But it's true. Once Stepan was on an expedition into inner Mongolia. His supplies ran out. He... killed one of his guides and ate him!"

"Vulpa—you're joking!"

"I'm telling you the truth. Stepan admitted it to me. Now you know why I shiver when he kisses me. You can understand why I have to fight back my screams when he makes love to me...."

It was unbelievable, of course. Burton couldn't credit such a fantastic tale. Not that it mattered to him, one way or the other. The main fact remained: Stepan Donnwyczi must be murdered, so that Vulpa would be free.

"How shall we work it?" Burton asked quietly.

"You—you mean you'll go through with it?"

"Yes."

"Oh-h-h... my love... my love!" She entwined her arms about Burton's neck and pulled him close; parted her lips over his mouth. Sultry, scalding sensations ripped through him. His embrace crushed her, so that her swollen white breasts were squeezed into flat cushions upon his chest. His palms traversed the planes of her back; and his fingers dug into the smooth, resilient flesh. He kissed her again, and it seemed almost that her lips probed his very soul. Ripples danced through her flesh as her slim figure writhed in the fervent passion of his embrace.

He noticed his own trembling and knew that he was nervous, jumpy, overwrought. He told himself that it was because of the consuming yearning that seethed in his blood. Never before had any woman aroused him as intensely as Vulpa. Yet there was a curious quality to her ardor; an undercurrent almost of savagery. Her eyes were narrowed, cat-like; for a moment her teeth were razor-sharp on his cheek. He had an abrupt, vague foreboding of evil; it seemed to emanate from her too-white flesh....

That was because she had asked him to kill her husband, he decided. And what of it? He knew, suddenly, that he would be willing to murder a hundred men to make sure of her love. She was worth it. He looked down at the taut hemispheres of her perfumed breasts, partially revealed where the negligee had slithered open. God, she was beautiful...!

An insane frenzy gripped him. He crushed her to him again, clamped his mouth roughly upon her lips. She moaned in what seemed a reciprocal fury of ecstasy and suddenly became limp....

Later, she smiled languorously at him and said: "It will be very easy. You will come home with me—now. For dinner. I have some poison already bought. You will put it in Stepan's wine.... But you must be sure to get the charm away from him first."

"Charm?"

She shrugged. "It is nothing. Just a foolish superstition of mine. Of course there is nothing to it. But...well, for safety, I would prefer—" Her voice died away in a whisper.

"I don't understand," Burton said.

"Stepan will explain. He... always does." She slipped her arm through his. "Come, my darling. We must go. It is late."

Burton was puzzled about this talk of a charm; but he was unable to pry anything further out of Vulpa as they taxied to her apartment. She was oddly silent during the journey.

But she assumed an air of carefree gayety the instant she entered her own front door. She hummed a weird, minor tune as she drew Burton into the living-room. "Stepan!" she called out lightly.

"We have a dinner guest!"

Stepan Donnwyczi slowly arose from the depths of an easy chair. "Oh, hello, Burton," he said. He was a tall, sallow man whose pointed ears and black brows gave him a Satanic appearance despite his friendly smile. "Glad to have you." He thrust out his hand.

Burton shook it perfunctorily. This was the man he intended to murder—tonight. He studied Donnwyczi, and wondered at his own utter calmness. It was odd that he felt no abhorrence for what he intended to do. Stepan Donnwyczi was alive, now; in a few hours he would be dead—and Burton would be responsible for that death. Yet his conscience did not stir in revolt against the prospect.

He remembered that girl—one of the many who had loved him—who had killed herself because of him. He'd felt no grief over her, either. He had been quite dispassionate and callous. He was the same way now. Soon he would be a murderer. Well, what of it?

As a matter of truth, Stepan and Vulpa seemed far more nervous at the dinner table than Burton did. Burton noticed that neither of them ate very much, barely tasting their food and then pushing it aside. Vulpa's jumpy nerves were logical enough, Burton thought, since she knew she would shortly be a self-made widow; but why should Stepan be distrait? Could he have guessed what was planned for him…?

As if in answer to Burton's unspoken question, the man spoke unexpectedly after the table had been cleared and cigarettes lighted. He looked at Burton and said: "Are you in love with my wife by any chance?"

Burton felt the blood draining from his face; he had to fight to keep control of his voice. "Are you joking?" he managed to say, finally. "I've only known you and Vulpa a month…."

"Other men have fallen in love with her in less time than that," Stepan smiled thinly. "Haven't they, my dear?" His piercing eyes bored into those of his wife.

She flushed uncomfortably. "Can I help it if I am… attractive, Stepan?"

"No. Of course you can't." Donnwyczi turned back to Burton. "She speaks the truth. She has rather a weird fascination for men. She puts them under a sort of—spell, perhaps you'd call it. Some of her lovers have even tried to murder me."

Burton almost sprang from his chair. "Really, old man—aren't you going a bit too far?"

"Not at all. You're my friend… aren't you? Then why shouldn't I speak frankly to you? Not that I think *you'd* try to kill me. That would be most foolish of you. *I can't be killed.*"

Burton's fists were clenched at his sides. "What do you mean by that?" he tried to be casual.

"I mean that I am impervious to murder—as quite a number have found out to their sorrow. Death strikes swiftly at those who attempt to kill me." Stepan looked at Vulpa. "How many of your lovers have died in an effort to do me in, my dear?"

"I—I—"

"You don't remember? Ah, but I do. Exactly five." Chuckling, Stepan withdrew a small object from his pocket and placed it on the table. It was a tiny bronze idol, hideously fashioned. "That is my charm, Burton. The thing that protects me."

Burton was sweating. "Charm—?"

"Yes. I picked it up in Mongolia. It was given to me by a man whom I later… ate."

"Good God—!" Burton sprang to his feet. "I—I think I'll be going. I just remembered an engagement—"

Stepan Donnwyczi grinned almost mischievously. "But no! You can't leave yet. Vulpa is going to dance for us. Aren't you, my sweet?"

Vulpa shivered. "No—please—"

"But I insist. We must entertain our guest. I'm sure he'll enjoy your dancing. Start the gramophone. Quickly!" The man's voice

*"You really want me
to commit murder?"
he asked.*

grew stingingly insistent, like the cracking of a whiplash.

Vulpa cringed at his tone, meekly placed a record on the machine and set the mechanism in motion. Then, before Burton's astounded eyes, she unhooked the snap-catches of her frock and slowly disrobed, there in the middle of the room.

Presently, nude save for her step-ins and bandeau of black lace she began to sway in languorous time to the rhythmic beat of barbaric music issuing from the phonograph's throat.

At first, Burton was filled with bewilderment that her husband would force her to display herself in such fashion. Then, gradually, a tide of dark anger welled up in him. No wonder she hated and feared Stepan Donnwyczi! The man was an inhuman monster who held her in psychic bondage; who compelled her to do his bidding, no matter how fantastic.

What was the nature of this thralldom she endured? What hold had Stepan on her soul? Asking himself these things, Burton no longer had any desire to leave; no longer felt any fear of Donnwyezi. He must murder the man—and the sooner the better. He must free Vulpa.

She was dancing with wild abandon now, gyrating to the pounding beat of drums and pirouetting to the wail of strange reed instruments. Slowly her hands moved across her bosom; her shoulders seemed to dip and her arms took on a snaky, undulant crawling movement that blended with the swaying of her lyric hips. Shame was scrawled on her delicate face as she displayed the gorgeous splendor of her meagrely clad body before the eyes of her husband and her sweetheart....

As she danced, her eyes burned into Burton's. She seemed to be trying to tell him something. She looked quickly at the barren dinner-table, then stared at him again. Abruptly he caught her meaning. Stepan Donnwyczi's miniature idol-charm—

It lay there on the polished table-surface, diabolically ugly in its tiny bronze workmanship. Stepan was watching his wife; his attention was not on the little idol. Stealthily Burton picked up the thing. Unnoticed, he jammed it into his pocket. Stepan apparently didn't see the move.

Then the phonograph record stopped. Vulpa turned, reached for her dress. Over her shoulder, she asked, "May I stop dancing now, Stepan?"

"Yes. Of course. And thank you for the splendid performance, my sweet." He grinned sardonically at Burton. "Do you not think Vulpa very beautiful, old fellow?"

"Er... of course. But—"

"But you object to her displaying herself before a comparative stranger, eh? You Americans have rather peculiar ideas about such matters. In the Carpathians, where I was born, a man takes pride in his wife's loveliness. A matter of ego, perhaps. Ah, well...." He yawned elaborately. "Shall we go into the library and have a spot of port?"

Vulpa spoke quickly. "Yes. Of course. Perhaps Mr. Burton will help me to bring it in—" She was sliding into her frock as she said it.

Stepan chuckled. "An excellent idea, my dear." He went from the room; and he seemed to have completely forgotten his little charm-idol. At least he didn't look for it on the table.

Burton sprang toward Vulpa. "We can't go through with it!" he whispered harshly. "He's wise to us—he knows—"

She plucked at his sleeve; drew him into the pantry. "He suspects nothing. He always acts that way when we have guests. He takes delight in shaming me, humiliating me, accusing me of being... wanton...."

"You mean—there's no truth in what he said about other lovers?"

Her green eyes flamed with inner flickers of light, weirdly. She squared her shoulders with a proud, arrogant gesture, so that her full-blown bosom was thrust boldly forward against the restraint of her frock. She had re-fastened her dress only partly in front, and Burton could now see the taut whiteness of flesh that peeked aluringly out of the low-cut vee. "I have loved no one except you!" she told him evenly.

Her fragrance and her nearness again made him tremble with emotion for her. Once more he felt that dark rip-tide of eagerness which had possessed him back in his own apartment. His arms went out to her; he caught her in a crushing embrace. "I wouldn't care if there had been a thousand other men!" he growled harshly. "I still love you...!"

Fluidly, she melted against him for a single instant. She gave him her lips in a moist, fervent kiss that seared into his very soul.... Then she drew back, gasping. "No! No more... until you have carried out your end of the pact!" she whispered.

And she handed him a little packet of white, crystalline powder.

He stared at it. "The poison—for Stepan's wine?"

"Yes."

"You're sure it will work!"

"Very sure."

"But—but suppose he guesses the truth—?"

"He won't; because he thinks he is protected by that horrible little idol."

Burton stiffened. He had forgotten the charm. Now he drew it from his pocket. "Surely he doesn't really believe in such rot!"

"But he does. And I know he has not missed it. Tonight was the first time I have ever seen him lay it aside, even for a moment. It is so much a part of his life that he has completely forgotten he hasn't got it with him. I know. I can tell."

Burton's lips were grim; his eyes hard. "So, if he thinks he still has the charm, he'll drink his poisoned wine without question?"

"Yes. Give it to me," Vulpa took the tiny bronze figure and thrust it into the wine-closet, out of sight. "I'll hide it here."

Then she got out three stemmed glasses and a bottle of tawny port. Two of the glasses were rimmed with blue enamel; the third was banded with red. She filled all three with the blood-red wine; then gestured to the glass with the crimson rim. "Pour the poison into this one, my lover."

Burton obeyed, emptying the contents of the packet into the dark wine. The crystalline white powder melted, dissolved, and was gone.

Vulpa smiled, her sharp white teeth gleaming. She placed the three glasses on a silvered tray.

"Turn off the pantry light."

Burton flicked the switch. "All set," he said steadily.

He heard her sharp whisper: "Be sure to give him the red glass. Then drink your own wine quickly—so that he will follow suit." In the darkness, she thrust the silvered tray forward. "Here; you carry it…."

Stepan awaited them in the library. He crushed out his cigarette as they entered; smiled from the depths of his easy-chair. "Ah, the wine!" he said softly. Then, casting a quizzical glance at Burton: "And did you enjoy Vulpa's kisses, old chap?"

Burton almost dropped the tray. He scowled. "I don't know what you mean. I wouldn't—"

"But there is lipstick on your mouth, you know. And what of it? I cannot blame you. Vulpa is very… lovely."

Anger choked Burton's gullet. "See here—!"

"Ah, you are vexed. Forgive me. Look; I will show you that I bear no ill-feelings toward this woman who is my wife." Stepan surged to his feet and caught Vulpa by the shoulders; drew her into his arms. As if to taunt the man who watched, he clamped his mouth upon her lips, mashing them brutally and kissing her with a savage intensity.

She struggled to get away from him; but his embrace tightened. Burton wanted to drop the tray and throw himself at Donnwyczi; batter the fellow to a pulp. But he dared not. Such a move would destroy all his plans; spoil his murder scheme. He must pretend to be unmoved, so that Stepan would drink the poisoned wine.

But Stepan did not tire for a long while. He ran his hands over his wife's shoulders; caught and ripped at the frock; tore it downward almost to her waist. She staggered back away from him, gasped, then as Stepan grabbed her again, she fought to cover the snowy domes of her bosom with the tatters of the frock. Her husband chuckled and shoved her hands away. He kissed her on the throat. With a frantic writhing she jerked free, stumbled backward until she lost her balance and fell across the divan behind her. The hem of her skirt flurried upward to disclose creamy thighs….

Stepan stood over her, breathing hoarsely. He smiled sardonically. "Are you ashamed to have me make love to you, my sweet? But remember I am your husband!"

"Please—before Mr. Burton—!"

"Oh. So that is it. But I am doing this for his benefit. I wish to show him that I forgive you for giving him your kisses…."

Burton stepped forward. "Listen, Donnwyczi! Hasn't this gone just about far enough!"

"Ah… perhaps yes. I keep forgetting that you Americans are unused to the ways of the Balkan people." Stepan turned from

She had killed herself because of him, and he had felt no grief.
That was a kind of murder; now he would kill again!

the divan, shrugged. Vulpa swayed to her feet, adjusted her skirt, drew the torn frock-bodice over her swelling bosom.

Then she smiled bitterly. "You must forgive Stepan, Mr. Burton. This is his idea of humor."

Burton frowned. "I don't like it."

Donnwyczi's lips curled in a wolfish grin. "Accept my apologies, old fellow. Come—let us drink to a better understanding a… more *internal*… friendship."

Now was the time! Burton's pulses began to hammer and throb as he held out the tray with its three brimming glasses of port. In a moment, this whole mad farce would be over. Stepan Donnwyczi would be dead. Then Vulpa would be free and her kisses, all her love, would be Burton's alone….

She took one of the blue-rimmed glasses from his tray. Completely indifferent to the murder he was about to commit, Burton extended the tray toward Stepan, so holding it that the red-decorated glass was foremost. Would Stepan accept it without question...? Would he take the poisoned wine without suspecting...?

He did. He lifted the crimson-rimmed wine-glass without hesitation; raised it toward his lips. "To our appetites!" he toasted.

Burton's fingers closed about the remaining glass. He drank the port in one gulp. And then his eyes widened horribly.

He stared at Stepan Donnwyczi. The man was sipping his wine with apparent enjoyment—and he was toying with a tiny bronze object in his left hand—

The idol-charm!

Burton's mouth went dry. "That—that thing—*where did you get it?*" he rasped.

Stepan smiled; his eyes held a peculiar, feral glitter. "My charm? Ah, friend Burton; did I fail to tell you all its qualities? Whenever someone steals it from me, it finds its way back into my pocket. That is part of its magic. I cannot lose it by theft; and while I own it, *I cannot be murdered.* For example—there is no poison in this wine I drink. Does that startle you? It should not, because I told you that you could not kill me. I also told you of the five men who have died for trying to murder me—as you are now dying!"

The room seemed to be swirling about Burton; daggers of agony were plunging through his belly and slicing upward toward his heart. "My God—my God—*I've poisoned myself—!*"

"Shall we call it suicide, my friend?" Stepan asked ironically.

But Burton did not hear the question. He had slumped to the floor. He was quite dead.

Stepan laughed, and the sound was like the ululation of a wolf. Another laughter, higher, more keening, blended with his own. Vulpa glided toward him, her red lips curling away from sharp white teeth. "The charm—the fool believed it, my Stepan!" she shrilled. "He thought it got back to you through thin air from the pantry where I hid it!"

Stepan caught her in his arms. "He didn't guess that I had a duplicate in my pocket all the time!"

She snuggled against him. "Nor did he suspect that I switched trays on him in the darkness of the pantry—so that *he* would drink the poison instead of you!"

"Ah…. But you cannot say we murdered him, my sweet. He caused his own death. He drank his wine voluntarily, did he not?"

"Yes. Yes. It was suicide, clearly, my beloved husband…. Stepan I am hungry…."

"And I, too. It has been a long time since you lured the last one, eh?"

"A month or more, Stepan…."

"Then let us feast, before the poison soaks through into his flesh…." From his pocket, Donnwyzci drew a clasp-knife. He opened it and handed it to his wife.

She laughed again as she hunkered down on the floor alongside Burton's corpse. Her mouth slavered as she sliced away at the dead man's clothing. Saliva fell from her blood-red lips and pointed teeth as she hacked at the lifeless body beside her, her hands dripping with the blood of the man who loved her fatally.

Stepan sat on the floor beside her, his eyes madly agleam, his mouth drooling at the sight of the blood and mutilated flesh. Together, the Donnwyczis laughed, and laughed again at the monstrous joke they had played on this latest of their victims.

HARLEY L. COURT

LORELEI OF LYNNWOLD LIGHT

One by one they died, in the sealed beacon-room of the lighthouse. No human hand could have murdered them... and nothing could have saved them from the siren of this death castle in the sea.

*T*here *was no* moon. Low, scudding clouds were gray shrouds that blanketed the dark sky; and beyond the high cliffs of Lynnwold, a sighing surf nursed at the teats of the rocky shore. The smell of the salt sea was in the midnight air; and somewhere in the dim distance I heard the harsh, mournful cry of a night-flying gull, thrice repeated.

The gull's cry waked me from uneasy dreaming. Then, on the heels of that faint and disturbing sound, there came an imperative knocking on the front door of my cliff-top cottage.

It seemed as though the wings of some dark presentiment brushed my cheeks as I arose from my bed to answer that insistent summons. I lighted a lantern and moved slowly toward the door. Even as my hand reached forth toward the heavy bolt, the knocking sounded again, sharp and demanding.

I opened the door.

A creeping tendril of fog curled ecto-plasmic tentacles toward me from the outer darkness. And then I saw the man who had knocked. He wore a thick pea-jacket over his blue uniform, and upon his left breast a gold badge gleamed. His face was strangely pale in the flare of my lantern, and when he spoke his voice held a flat timbre that rasped in his throat. "Are you Con Clinton, the new Inspector of Lighthouse Service for this district?" he asked me.

"Yes," I told him.

"I am Captain Blaine of the Lynnwold police. I came to tell you that Lynnwold Light has gone out."

His words sent a sudden icy fear down my spine. "Good God!" I whispered. "You don't suppose it's another... death?"

"I don't know," he answered me. "But I'm going out there to find out. And I thought you might wish to go along."

"I do!" I said quickly. And as I flung myself into my clothes, my mind raced back over what I had already learned about Lynnwold Light. My thoughts encompassed the two previous tragedies that had taken place in that bleak and isolated beacon-house; mysterious, inexplicable tragedies that had both been marked by the extinguishing of Lynnwold Light itself....

Lynnwold Lighthouse was built upon the foundation of a rock that thrust itself, like a scabrous sore, out of the sea six miles from the cliffs of the village. When the waves ran high—as they frequently do in that reef-strewn region—it was impossible to approach the Light in any sort of craft. Which meant that most of the time Dan Beucher, the keeper of the Light, was a prisoner cut off from all human contact. His was a job I did not envy.

But Dan Beucher never seemed to mind his isolation. Content in the companionship of his young, yellow-haired wife, he seemed almost to resent any intrusion. Time after time he had protested because the Service insisted that an assistant light-keeper be stationed with him to divide the duties of the job. Dan Beucher maintained that he could handle the Light by himself; that he wanted no helper.

And as though some dark, mysterious force were backing up Beucher's arguments, two assistants had died weird, impossible deaths in the past few months.

I say impossible, because that is true. Two men had died. Had been murdered. Yet the manner of their passing had been such that no finger of suspicion could be laid on Dan Beucher or his yellow-haired young wife. On the death of the first of Beucher's assistants, Beucher had been brought before a court of inquiry.

But it had been proven so conclusively that the light-keeper could not have done the killing that Beucher had been released forthwith.

Shortly thereafter, a second assistant had been murdered in precisely the same manner in which his predecessor met death. And now, for the third time, Lynnwold Light had gone out... even as it had been extinguished on two other sinister occasions....

Dressed at last, I pulled a heavy coat over my clothing and went out to the waiting captain of police. Together we descended the rocky path that led to the sea's calm edge. Captain Blaine had a broad-beamed motor-launch waiting at the end of Lynnwold wharf. I took the tiller as he started the craft's motor. We headed

There was the mysterious lighthouse— in which three men had been murdered!

forth over the smooth swells in the dark direction of the lighthouse where no light showed.

Over the steady cough of the engine, I began to query Captain Blaine. "These murders that took place in Lynnwold Light—just what happened to each case?" I asked him.

His voice held a chilled, icy gravity as he answered me. "Both times, the assistant was found at the very top of the lighthouse tower—inside the glassed-in beacon-chamber. In each case, the dead man had bolted the trap-door of the compartment, locking himself in. And both times, the murdered man's head had been blown open by a charge of buck-shot fired at murderously close range."

"The shots could not have been fired from any place outside the windows of the light?" I asked.

Blaine shook his head morosely. "No. The walls of the lighthouse are sheer and smooth. No living man could scale them from the outside. It would be physically impossible."

"There is no possible way to reach the beacon-chamber except by means of the ladder that leads upward inside the tower itself?"

"There is no way."

"And what of the murder weapon?"

"No trace was ever found, in either case."

I was silent for a long while. Then I asked another question. "Could a shotgun have been discharged from a passing airplane?"

"Certainly not!" Blaine snapped irritably. "Don't you suppose we considered that possibility? In the first place, a plane couldn't fly that close to the light; and if it did, how could the flyer take careful aim as he passed the beacon? I tell you, the shots were fired so close to the murdered men that the marks of powder-burns showed on their clothing."

"And in each case, the charge of shot also extinguished the light itself?"

"Exactly."

Ere I could question him further, Captain Blaine snapped on the powerful beam of a search-light at the bow of the launch. The thick white finger of illumination probed at the darkness, like a surgeon pulling open the edges of a black wound. And there, dead ahead of us in the night, lay the gray, sea-stained walls of Lynn-wold Lighthouse, looming out of the sea.

As best I could, I guided the launch toward a precarious landing at the edge of the jutting rocks which formed the foundation of that ominous stone tower. Patches of sea-moss, like green scabs, clung to the sheer sides of the structure; and I could see that Captain Blaine had been correct in what he had told me. No living thing could scale those straight, slippery walls to reach the glassed-in light-compartment at the top. It would have been utterly impossible.

We fastened the launch with a strong line. Then we leaped upon the wave-washed landing and approached the entrance to the lighthouse. The door opened before our faces. From somewhere within the dank, stone tower I heard a heavy pounding, as of wood against metal. *Thud—thud—thud!* the sound echoed and reverberated with hollow regularity, like the booming of a weird drum.

Then I looked at the person who had opened the door.

I drew a sharp breath of surprise; for I had never seen Dan Beucher's wife before. Now, as my eyes encompassed her frail beauty, I suddenly realized that never in my life had I seen a woman of such surpassing loveliness.

She was dressed in some light, clinging material; and as a gust of abrupt wind eddied against her, her dress flattened against the feminine curves of her body, silhouetting the rounded outlines of her well-formed breasts and the slim gracefulness of her legs and hips and thighs. Her golden hair streamed about her shoulders in the breeze, framing her oval face in a glinting aura. Her eyes were deep blue, long-lashed; her mouth was a red gash in the whiteness of her features, poppy-crimson, passion-tempting. She recognized Captain Blaine. "Thank God you've come!" she whispered tremulously.

"Where is your husband?" Blaine barked the question.

"He—he's upstairs, at the head of the ladder, trying to break in through the trap-door. Trying to get into the beacon-chamber...."

"And the assistant?"

The girl paled. "He's... inside the top of the tower... locked in... just like the others...."

Blaine leaped forward. I followed him. A winding iron staircase led upward around the inner walls of the structure. Our flying footsteps resounded hollowly as we raced upward. We passed a landing that gave access to the living-quarters occupied by Beucher and his wife. Beyond it, a steel-runged ladder led straight up. Above our heads, the pounding commenced again. *Thud— thud—thud!* like rumbling thunder.

"Beucher! Beucher, up there!" Blaine raised his voice.

The regular, metronome-like pounding ceased. A harsh voice floated downward. "Who is it?"

"It's Blaine of the police. And Mr. Clinton, your district inspector, is with me. We're coming up."

Blaine and I ascended toward the light of a flickering lantern far above. And then, at the very top of the ladder, where it ended against a closed iron trap-door overhead, I saw Dan Beucher.

He was a small man, stoop-shouldered and heavily lined. He held a heavy wooden beam in his hands, and he had been pounding with it against the locked trap-door over his head. Now he stared at us in the yellow lantern's rays. "You—you noticed that the light was out?" he said thickly.

"That's what brought us out here!" Captain Blaine snapped. "What's happened?"

"I—I don't know. About an hour ago, I heard a shot. It was—was just like those other two times…." Beucher shuddered. "I raced up here to the top of the ladder and found the trap-door bolted. I've been trying to smash it open—"

Blaine turned to me. "Lend a hand, Clinton." I seized hold of the heavy wooden beam that Beucher had been using as a battering-ram. Blaine also gripped it; and Beucher retained his own hold on the heavy piece of wood. All three of us, with concerted effort, smashed the beam's broad end upward against the trap-door above us. Under our combined strength, three blows sufficed. I heard a splintering sound over us, on the other side of the trap-door. The thick steel barrier gave way.

Blaine shoved the trap-door upward. It opened with a clanging clatter that reechoed weirdly through the damp recesses of the lighthouse tower. At the police captain's heels, I drew myself up into the pitch-dark beacon-chamber.

Dan Beucher entered last, carrying his flickering yellow lantern. "My God!" I whispered harshly as I stared.

On the steel floor of the constricted, glassed-in chamber lay the body of a man, grotesque in sudden death. He was sprawled face-forward; and when Blaine turned the corpse over, I saw that it had no face! The man's features had been torn apart and obliterated in a welter of bloody, shredded flesh. The top of his skull had been ripped off by a charge of shot fired from within two or three feet at the most!

The lenses of the Light had been shattered and broken by that demoniac murder-blast; and the three huge electric bulbs had been smashed into a million shards of fine, scattered glass. I looked

Never in my life had I seen a woman of such perfect beauty, such surpassing loveliness.

about me. The walls of the beacon-chamber were panes of thick plate-glass, well-cleaned and polished. I noticed that one of the panes had been slid back upon its grooves, leaving an opening not more than six inches wide.

"The shot must have been fired through this opening!" I cried. I leaped toward the spot I had noticed; slid the glass window all the way open. I stared outward, downward. And then I realized the impossibility of my theory. Outside the opened pane, the sheer walls of the lighthouse tower swept downward into the black sea, moss-covered and slime-slippery with the dampness of the sea and the night. No living thing could have scaled that rounded and precipitous wall; and there was no dangling rope up which a man might haul himself.

No; there was no possible way of reaching the beacon-chamber at the top of the lighthouse tower, save by means of the ladder on the inside of the structure. And yet—there was a dead man lying on the circular chamber's steel wall; lying in a gory welter of blood and oozing brains. For some inexplicable reason, he had locked himself inside the chamber—as though seeking to protect himself from dire misfortune. And now he was dead. Murder had overtaken him here in his locked refuge....

I saw the thick bit of wood that the man had used to fasten the trap-door from the inside. It was a solid timber—a two-by-four; and it had been slipped through two hasps—the one hasp on the top of the trap-door, the other on the beacon-chamber's steel flooring. Of course that wooden bolt was splintered and broken now, where the force of our battering-ram against the underside of the trap-door had cracked it in twain. A tiny bit of string dangled around the longer of the two splintered pieces. I turned my attention to the rest of the chamber, searching for some trace of the shotgun that had fired the murder-charge. But there was no shred of evidence that a weapon had ever been in that constricted place.

Dan Beucher sobbed a croaking oath. "Dammit, I've told them not to send an assistant to help me here on Lynnwold Light! The place is hexed—bewitched! And every man they send me will meet this same fate—"

"Are you not afraid for yourself, Beucher?" I asked him.

He shook his shaggy head, and his unkempt brows Drew together doggedly. "No!" he answered me. "Whatever it is that kills 'em—it won't bother me! It never has, and it never will! That's why I say leave me alone here on the Light. I can handle it. Just me and my wife!"

I smiled grimly. "It's beginning to look as though you might get your wish, Beucher. I doubt whether I could hire another assistant for you, in the light of what has happened to the last three."

Beucher's eyes gleamed in the yellow glow of the lantern. "I can handle the job myself. I've told 'em so, time after time!"

By then, Captain Blaine had finished his inspection of the chamber. "No clues!" he said shortly, bitterly. "There's nothing to do but carry this corpse back to the mainland and commence another investigation. Not that it'll get us anywhere!" he added harshly.

I helped the police official carry that gruesome, mutilated dead body down the iron ladder, out to Blaine's broad-bottomed launch. Blaine looked at me. "What do you intend doing, Clinton?"

"I'm staying here the balance of the night," I answered him. "You can come out in the launch and pick me up in the morning, if you will."

He eyed me narrowly. "You're not afraid to stay here?"

I smiled. "No. I'm not afraid," I told him. But deep in my heart I knew that I was lying. Because I was afraid. Some sinister miasma of mystery, of evil, of ominous danger, seemed to hover and lurk over and around every corner of Lynnwold Lighthouse. And yet I knew it was my duty to stay there; and in spite of my unvoiced, vaguely-sensed fears, I determined to do my duty.

Captain Blaine shrugged his heavy shoulders. "You know what you're doing, I guess," he said slowly. He offered me his hard hand. "Good luck!"

I returned his well-meaning, well-wishing grip. Shortly there-after, his launch put away from the rocky base of the lighthouse and was swallowed in darkness. I returned to the top of the tower, where Dan Beucher was busy installing new electric bulbs and new lenses in the shattered light. In a few moments, Lynnwold Light was once more darting its warning beam to unwary mari-ners, across the oily black waters of the reef-strewn sea.

At long last, he finished his task. Together we went back down to the living-quarters which he shared with his yellow-haired wife. The girl herself was nowhere in evidence; had apparently gone back to bed. Beucher led me to a small room. "This is where the assistants have slept. It's the only hospitality I can offer you," he said to me.

I nodded. "Thank you. I'll turn in and try to grab forty winks," I answered. "Call me if anything… happens…."

His eyes held a strange, affrighted look; and he refused to meet my gaze. I left him standing there, and went into the room where I was to sleep.

Divesting myself of hat and topcoat, I threw myself across the mussed bed—a bed that had been occupied not long before by a man who was now foully murdered. I closed my eyes, giving my mind over to the sinister problem of the mysterious death which struck out of nowhere, here in this isolated spot. The macabre, fantastic unreality of it was like a spine-chilling nightmare, unbelievable and yet terrifyingly true.

Through the darkness, I could hear the whispering slither of swells parting around the base of the lighthouse, hissing liquidly against the scabrous rocks. Directly below me, the subdued chuffing of a gasoline generator commenced as it started automatically upon its task of charging the batteries that supplied the current which fed the Light at the top of the tower.

I lay there, silent, for a long time. And then something disturbed me. I turned—and perceived that the door of my room was slowly opening on well-oiled, silent hinges.

I sat upright, staring. Through the darkness, a ghostly shape was approaching my bed. I felt the short hairs rise at the back of my neck, and my muscles seemed to creep like crawling worms. Then a faint fragrance, somehow strange and exotic, was wafted to my nostrils. The ghost-like form was nearing me. Abruptly I realized that it was a woman—a woman clad only in a flowing, thin nightgown. It was Dan Beucher's slender, fascinating, yellow-haired wife.

She leaned over me in the darkness. Her golden hair fell in softly-silken strands near my face. Her perfume stirred strange desires within my suddenly-throbbing veins, and her nearness was like a warm fire. "What do you want?" I whispered.

"I'm afraid!" she answered me tremulously. "I'm afraid. Dan is asleep, and I'm afraid!" I felt the softness of her body brushing against my own.

"Is something... wrong?" I whispered tensely.

"I don't know. But I feel a terrible, terrifying fear. And you are so young—so strong—I had to come—" Abruptly she flung herself upon me, clinging to me with her bare, rounded arms. Tiny darts of electrical desire surged within me! I grabbed her and held her slender, vibrant body in my arms.

She lay quiescent, as though my strength had banished her fear. In the darkness, scarcely realizing what I was doing, I sought for her red lips with my mouth. And she accepted my questing kiss willingly, hotly.

I felt her lips open wide against my own. Her fire-hot tongue stole boldly forth, moistly, passionately. Her white, sharp teeth clamped down over my mouth; it seemed as though she were seeking to draw out my soul—

The blood quickened and raced through my veins in surging vortexes of aroused passion. Though I knew what I did was monstrously wrong, it seemed as though I could not help myself. I pulled at the straps of her thin, sheer nightgown—pulled them downward, over her arms. Her bared breasts were hot and throbbing and firmly-soft to my exploring fingers, like rounded mounds of enchantment and desire. My palms flattened those mollescent hillocks of flesh.

Abruptly I came to my senses; realized that I was with another man's wife.... I drew back, trembling with inhibited longings that battered against the moral barriers within my brain. But Beucher's wife would have none of my scruples. She fastened herself to me, battening upon my lips with hot ardor that left me gasping. She panted sharply, commandingly. "Hold me—kiss me!" Her bare arms entwined themselves about my neck, drawing my head toward her quivering and naked bosoms.

"But your husband—"

"Is asleep. He'll never know!"

Even while I cursed myself for cuckolding Dan Beucher, I could not resist the hot desires that flowed through my veins; could not withstand the flaming passions that leaped through my body at the nearness of this yellow-haired girl whose half-naked body lay so close to mine. Her breasts set me afire. My hands sank into those twin, melon-like soft mounds. I kissed her mouth, her shoulders, her warm throat. Her slim fingers were burrowing beneath my shirt, stroking the muscles of my panting chest.

Savagely I crushed her undulating body close to me. With my hands I caressed the nubile curves of her hips through the thin silken nightgown. The hem of the garment had twisted upward above her knees, and my palms encountered naked, quivering thigh-flesh.

Later, she lay still in my arms. Her yellow hair streamed about my face, smothering me in redolent softness. Her slim fingers toyed playfully about my lips—

She stiffened. *"Listen!"* she gasped.

I heard soft footfalls outside the closed door of my room. "Your husband!" I whispered tensely.

She leaped from the bed, hauled at me until I was standing beside her in the darkness. "God!" she whispered harshly. "He'll find us here together! He'll—he'll kill us both—!"

Then, from without my door, Dan Beucher's voice rose in a cracked bellow. "Clinton—open up! I know you've got my wife in there! Open up, I say! I want to talk to you, man!"

Beucher's yellow-haired wife pulled at my arm. "Hurry—for God's sake!" she hissed desperately. "Here—here's another door! It leads out upon the landing inside the tower!" She flung herself at the closed portal, yanked it open, dragged me through it. "Run—up the ladder into the beacon-chamber! Lock yourself in until I can get him quieted!" she pleaded.

I stopped dead in my tracks. "Go up to the beacon-chamber?" I whispered savagely. "And perhaps be murdered, even as those three assistants were killed—?"

"No—no! My husband killed those men! Killed them down here, and carried their bodies up to the top of the Light. He had some means of locking the trap-door, as though from the inside. But if you get up there before he does, you can bolt yourself in. You'll be safe from him—!" She was pushing me toward the ladder; and something of her terror communicated itself to my veins. I leaped upward, ascending the ladder's iron rungs. I reached the trap-door, flung it open. Below me I heard Dan Beucher leaping out upon the landing. He was cursing, foully. "Clinton—come back down here!" he screamed. "Don't go into that beacon-chamber!"

But I paid him no heed. Desperately I drew myself up through the open steel trap-door; slammed the trap down after me. It fell home with a metallic clangor. I was alone in the beacon-chamber. The intense, blinding brilliance of Lynnwold Light stabbed at my eyes like white-hot fire, and the heat of the three huge, burning incandescent bulbs made the chamber seem like an oven in hell.

Below me, through the closed trap-door, I heard Dan Beucher laboring up the ladder. "Clinton!" he bellowed hoarsely. "Don't lock that trap! As you value your life, man, *don't bar it!*"

Then his wife's scream knifed past his voice, ululating, weird, terror-ridden. "Bar the trap-door! Bar it or—he'll kill you!"

I knew a single split-second of frozen immobility. I could hear, under my feet, the sound of a struggle as Beucher's yellow-haired wife grappled with him, tried to keep him from ascending further. I acted. I saw, at my feet, that broken wooden two-by-four which Blaine and I had split in twain when we had forced entrance into this chamber of horror, earlier that night. The longer of the two pieces could still be employed to bolt the hasps of the trap-door. I leaped toward it—

Leaped, and suddenly brought up short as my eyes beheld the black muzzle of a shotgun pointed directly at my face!

"God!" I cried out. I stared. The weapon was thrust in through a narrow slit in the circular glass sides of the beacon-room, where one thick pane had been slid back a little in its frame. The shotgun was balanced precariously upon the open ledge, its stock hanging out over the black sea far below. There was nothing behind it; no human hands held it trained at me. Outside the glass windows, there was nothing save the darkness of the night....

And then, abruptly, I saw the fiendish ingenuity of the trap.

A string led from the weapon's trigger to the piece of wood which I had almost picked up. Had I grabbed at that splintered two-by-four, jammed it through the hasps of the trap-door, the shotgun would have discharged its murderous load full into my skull!

Like a flash, I whipped off my belt. Below me, Beucher and his wife were still struggling on the ladder, as I could tell from the scuffling sounds. I leaped toward the shotgun, hooked a loop of my belt around its barrel, tightened the knot. I fastened the belt-buckle to a projecting nail. Then, keeping out of range of the gun's muzzle, I stepped aside and kicked at the piece of wood.

There was a roaring reverberation that deafened my ears in that restricted space; a flash of licking yellow flame; the shattering of glass as the lenses and incandescents of Lynnwold Light were splintered by the smashing charge of buckshot at close range.

In the sudden, intense blackness I leaped toward the shotgun's smoking muzzle. My fumbling fingers told me the truth of the story. The recoil of the discharged weapon had kicked it backward off the sill; and had it not been for the belt I had tied around the barrel, the gun would have hurled itself backward into the black waters far below. As it was, the gun hung suspended on the outside of the tower, dangling by my belt against the slimy walls of the lighthouse.

"Damn ye! Damn your foul soul to the fiends o' hell!" I heard Dan Beucher's rasping, madman's cry below me. "Ye've sent another one to his death! Ye insane, blood-thirsty nymphomaniac! Ye let them make love to ye—and then ye kill 'em! To keep ye out of an asylum, I brought ye here to this lonely spot; but because they insist on sending assistants out here to me, your foul work goes on! Ye fiend! Ye bloody she-devil out o' hell—"

The marrow froze in my veins. Then Dan Beucher's wife was the murderess! A lusting, maniacal killer—a woman who drank deep of passion from her victims, before she sent them to horrible death—!

I saw the whole thing now. The woman would love her intended victim; then, pretending fear of her perfectly harmless husband, she would send the doomed man up into the light-tower; tell him to bar himself in. Meanwhile she had set her shotgun-trap. And when the victim picked up a piece of wood to bar the trap-door, he would trip the weapon's hair-trigger....

And the murder-gun, having completed its deadly work, would recoil and kick itself into the sea, never to be found! Then there would be nothing but a dead body in that locked, inaccessible light-chamber—

I heard Beucher's wife laughing shrilly, insanely. "Another one!"

she gloated horribly. "Aye, another one! Dead! And what will you do about it, Dan Beucher?"

Savagely, I wrenched open the trapdoor and lowered myself from that black, circular room that might have been my death trap. "He won't need to do anything about it!" I shouted grimly. "Whatever there is to be done—I'll do!"

They were struggling upon the landing below me, Beucher and his wife. His clawing fingers had ripped the nightgown from her body, leaving her nude and beautiful with a hellish, seductive loveliness. Now, at the sound of my unexpected voice, they both sprang apart—stared up at me—

"God in heaven! I didn't kill him!" the woman wailed.

"And now ye'll hang!" Beucher sobbed. Suddenly, before I could reach him, he grabbed his wife in his arms. "I've protected ye this long. And I'll protect ye unto death!" he whispered as he kissed her open lips. Then he lifted her, whirled, started down the circular staircase toward the base of the lighthouse.

I broke after them in full pursuit. But Beucher was too swift for me. Before I had more than halfway gained the lower landing, he had flung himself with his burden out through the door of the lighthouse, out into the night. And when at last I reached that lower level and sprang out after him, he was poised on the rocky ledge that jutted into the swirling, inky sea.

"Beucher—stop!" I cried out. Compassion was in my heart—compassion for this man, and pity; for I knew the aching torment his soul had undergone because he loved a murderess. And he had tried to save me; had warned me not to bar the trap-door at the top of the tower. "Beucher—stop!" I cried again.

But his ears were deaf to my pleading. His yellow-haired wife was struggling in his arms; he held to her with grim finality. Then, before my widened eyes, he leaped—

Leaped into the sucking, swirling waters that slithered and whispered in the black darkness below Lynnwold Light. Leaped, with his wife still cradled in his arms, tenderly, like a little girl-child.... She screamed once, wetly, sickeningly. And then the water closed over their two heads, and it was as though Beucher and his wife had never been.

I sometimes wonder if she ever knew, before she died, the full extent of Dan Beucher's loyalty and his all-forgiving love.

JEROME SEVERS PERRY

MURDER FROM NOWHERE

The girl had come to him out of the night... and now death threatened them both. What awful secret would the little bronze coffin reveal?

Outside, a late autumn storm lashed at the night with black, lancing spates of rain and gashing daggers of lightning. Thunder crashed and rumbled and re-echoed in a devil's barrage, so that the very earth seemed to shake and quiver ominously.

John Bryant sat alone in the library of his cousin's country house, reading. Despite himself, he shivered a little, although the room was comfortably warm. In the great hearth beside him, a blazing log fire leaped, throwing weirdly-flickering shadows upon the shelf-lined walls. In the spectral, dancing light, the mounted animals on the shelves seemed almost to move and to have evil, unbidden life.

Dozens of them there were—stuffed beasts from the jungles of South America, venomous reptiles from hot tropic climes, snarling ape-heads and crouching monsters of sinister silence. There were even two or three shrunken, dessicated, leathery human heads—trophies from some nameless Ecuadorian headhunting tribe, gruesome and spine-chilling.

Again John Bryant stifled a queer shudder. His cousin and host was Dr. William Gaxton, the noted surgeon who had spent so many years south of the equator, and whose hobby was taxidermy. These motionless, mounted figures on the walls of the library

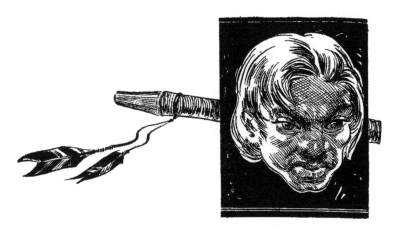

were examples of the surgeon's skill and his handiwork. And they filled John Bryant with a queer uneasiness.

John Bryant had arrived from an exploring trip in Central Asia only that afternoon, to visit his eminent cousin. Then it developed that Dr. Gaxton and his attractive brunette wife, Thora, had a theater engagement the same evening.

Of course John Bryant had refused to let them break the engagement, since his own arrival had been entirely unexpected. He had been perfectly content, he had told them, to remain alone in the house during their evening's absence.

But now he found himself vaguely regretting the decision, although he could not quite fathom the reason. There seemed to be a hovering atmosphere of brooding somberness about the house—a somberness heightened by the lashing storm outside. It was a curious, still weirdness that crept into John Bryant's veins like an omen of disaster.

Strangely, the feeling seemed to center about a small bronze casket, the size of a child's coffin, which rested upon a black onyx pedestal in one darkened, funereal corner of the library. What that bronze casket contained, John Bryant did not know. Its heavy lid was closed and clamped. But again and again he found his gaze wandering from the pages of his book, returning to that small, coffin-like thing—

What was that?

John Bryant tensed. Once again he heard the sound—a hurried,

frantically-importunate knocking upon the front door of the house. Knowing that he was alone, that there were no servants, he sprang to his feet, went to the door, threw it open.

At that same instant, a jagged, blazing scimitar of lightning stabbed an eye-blinding wound in the dark storm. In the sudden baleful light, John Bryant saw a woman—a girl—standing there in the fury of the wind-whipped rain. She was drenched to the skin, and she held a small, squirming bundle in her arms. She seemed timid, tired, frightened....

"I—I am so sorry to trouble you!" the girl gasped out faintly, with just the faintest trace of sibilant accent. "My—my automobile broke down, a mile up the road. I am alone with—with my baby. I wondered if you would allow me to use your telephone to call a garage?"

"Of course!" John Bryant smiled. "Come in."

He led her into the house, into the warm library. He perceived that the baby in her arms was covered in the folds of a raincoat— a raincoat which evidently the girl had taken from her own shoulders to protect her tiny burden from the lashing rain. Then Bryant looked at the girl herself.

Her beauty struck him like a blow to the heart. Damp, blue-black hair clung to her head and framed, with curling ringlets, the perfect olive-ivory oval of her face. Her eyes were dark liquid pools in which fear-shadows seemed to lurk; her mouth was poppy-red and made for kisses.

Bryant saw that her storm-soaked frock clung intimately to the exquisite contours of her small, feminine body, limning the girlish curves of her hips and the firm pointed breasts. Her ankles were slender, her legs delicately tapered.

With a start, Bryant came to himself. His staring survey of the girl's pulse-quickening charms had brought a blush to her olive cheeks. Apologetically he smiled and went toward the telephone. "I'll ring a garage for you," he said gently.

She nodded her thanks. Bryant un-forked the receiver, rattled the hook. But there was no life, no sound on the line. It was dead—evidently out of commission because of the raging storm.

Ruefully he replaced the telephone and faced his feminine visitor. "Sorry," he said. "The line seems to be out of order."

Her dark eyes clouded. "Oh!" she said in a half-whisper. "What will I do now?"

John Bryant smiled. "Stay here until the rain's over. I'll get you some brandy and a dry robe. You're drenched."

He went out of the library; and as he stepped through the door into the hallway, he had a sudden sensation that evil eyes were boring malefically into his back. He turned, swiftly: but the girl was facing away from him. She seemed to be staring toward a far corner of the library… toward that child's-sized coffin on its onyx pedestal….

He went to his room; returned, a few moments later, with his own flannel dressing-gown and a bottle of Hennessy. His eyes narrowed a little as he entered the library. The girl was still standing in the center of the room; but it almost seemed as though he had heard her running to the spot. Perhaps it was imagination, he told himself, but he got the vague impression that she had been in that darkened corner, examining the bronze casket….

But that was ridiculous, he forced himself to admit. Smiling, he poured a stiff drink of brandy and handed it to the girl. She accepted and drank it gratefully. Then she placed her baby on the divan and took John Bryant's flannel robe.

While he reluctantly turned his back, she unfastened her soaked frock and shrugged out of it. Beneath the dress, she wore nothing but sheer thin panties; and her unbrassiered breasts were firm and softly feminine. She donned the warm robe.

"Now you may turn," she said quietly.

Bryant faced her. She spread her wet dress on the fire-screen before the hearth; then she settled herself upon the divan, picked the baby up in her arms. From a pocket of the raincoat she withdrew a nursing-bottle half filled with milk; gave it to the infant. The child cooed and gurgled contentedly; made wet, sucking noises. As the girl leaned over her task, the robe fell away from her lovely breasts. John Bryant caught a glimpse of swelling, olive-white hillocks of nubile flesh, and his heart raced....

She looked at him; saw the direction of his gaze. She blushed and pulled the robe about her bosom. As though to make conversation, her eyes wandered about the shelf-lined room with its mounted trophies. "Your work, Dr. Gaxton?" she asked.

Bryant shook his head. "I'm not Dr. Gaxton. My name's Bryant—John Bryant. Dr. Gaxton is my cousin. I'm staying here with him for a short visit. The taxidermy is his."

The girl seemed just a little startled, a bit surprised. Her dark, penciled brows rose almost imperceptibly, and she seemed to catch her breath. Then she smiled, revealing twin rows of small, pearly teeth. "I have heard of Dr. Gaxton," she said. "He had the reputation of being a great surgeon in Ecuador—in Quito."

"You have been there?" Bryant asked.

She nodded. "It is my home."

So that accounted for her olive skin, her Latin loveliness, Bryant mused. And then once more he found himself wondering about the fear-shadows that seemed to lurk in her slumbrous eyes. It seemed as though the aura of evil which hovered over the house had been heightened since her arrival....

Then, abruptly, he heard the crunch of tires on the wet gravel driveway outside. That, probably, he thought, would be his cousin and his wife, returning from the theater. Bryant got to his feet.

"Pardon me a minute," he smiled at the brunette girl.

She nodded. Bryant left the library, went to the front door of the house, opened it wide.

A statuesque woman leaped from a parked sedan, ran across the porch and into the hallway. It was Thora, Dr. William Gaxton's wife. She was alone.

As she threw off her wet cloak, John Bryant looked at her. "Hello, Thora," he said. "Where's Bill?"

"He had an emergency call during the third act—had to leave. I came home alone. He'll follow later, in a cab."

Thora Gaxton was tall, lithe, full of a strange feline grace. Her dark hair gave startling contrast to the milky whiteness of her skin; and her features were beautiful with a cold, hard beauty. She had been Dr. Gaxton's nurse during the surgeon's years in South America; and later, Gaxton had married her. Now John Bryant saw that the decolletage of her evening gown was ultra-daring; her full, erect white breasts were audaciously disclosed. Oddly enough, she possessed no attraction for Bryant. She was too cold, too imperious. At that instant, it almost seemed as if he disliked her—although he could not tell why.

As she started past him toward the library, he said, "By the way, Thora, we've got visitors. A young South American girl and her baby. Her car broke down."

"South American girl?" Thora Gaxton rasped out harshly. She went pale. Then she ran toward the library. Bryant followed her, wondering.

They reached the library door. Over Thora's stiffened shoulder, John Bryant stared. A swift amazement filled him.

The olive-skinned girl, with the baby in her arms, was standing in the far corner, beside that small bronze casket on its onyx pedestal. She had evidently just opened the lid of the chest. Now, startled, she slammed it shut and whirled around. Her eyes were wide with sudden fright.

Momentarily, Thora Gaxton had frozen in her tracks. Now, suddenly, she leaped ahead; and her sharp fingernails clawed out—

"Open that casket and you die!"

The South American girl wailed faintly; eluded the older woman's rush; managed to deposit her baby on the divan. Then, before she could defend herself, Thora was upon her.

"Thora—what the devil—!" John Bryant yelled. He took a forward step; but he was too late to hold his cousin's wife back. Thora's hands had clutched at the younger woman's robe—had yanked the heavy garment from the girl's shoulders, exposing her body and her firm breasts....

"I'll teach you to come here and meddle!" Thora Gaxton snarled savagely. Then the girl managed to get free; ran cowering to a far corner. Thora started after her. And then a strange thing happened.

As John Bryant watched, his cousin's wife suddenly stiffened. Abruptly she choked out a terrified cry of fright and of pain. Her fingers clawed wildly at her left breast, ripped open the gown's decolletage so that her breasts were exposed, naked. Her eyes widened horribly.

John Bryant leaped toward Thora, saw a sudden greenish pallor spreading over her contorted features. Then she toppled and fell before he could catch her. She sprawled on the floor at his feet; writhed fantastically, grotesquely. Abruptly she stiffened and was still. Ominously still.

"God!" John Bryant rasped in his throat. He went to his knees beside the prone form of Thora Gaxton; rolled her over. Her eyes were wide, staring, glazing; the pupils were horribly dilated. There was a fleck of froth at her thin, pallid lips, and her tongue protruded like a thick, blood-stained gag....

Bryant's hand sought the woman's heart; pressed deeply into the flesh of her left breast. A cold chill crept down his spine.

"She's dead!" he whispered.

"D-dead?" the olive-skinned girl wailed. *"Por Dios*... no! No! It cannot be true...!"

"But it is true!" Bryant answered grimly. He stared down at Thora's lifeless, lovely corpse. And then his eyes narrowed.

There was a faint red mark over her left breast—a tiny, coagulated droplet of crimson. Already a greenish-blue hue—the hue of putrescence—was spreading in a circle under the milk skin, surrounding that droplet of blood!

Something familiar about the sight stirred a sudden memory, an abrupt knowledge within John Bryant's mind. He looked more closely—and saw what he had known must be there. Something glittered like a silver pin-point, deeply imbedded in the dead woman's bosom....

He sprang to his feet; stood unsteadily. "Thora was killed by a poisoned needle—a dart from a blow-gun!" he rasped. "I've been in the South American jungles often enough to recognize it for what it is!"

The olive-skinned girl went corpse-pale. *"Dios!"* she cried wildly. "You... you do not think that I... killed her...?"

"No. You couldn't have done it. I was watching you all the time. But that dart was blown from somewhere in this very room—!" Abruptly he raced toward the far corner, toward that bronze casket on its ivory pedestal. He searched the shadows. No lurking form hovered anywhere in the library. There was no one save himself and the frightened South American girl....

"*Madonna mia!*" she whispered. "I did not know—I did not realize—"

But Bryant was not listening to her hysterical babblings. Like a flash he hurled himself at the windows; but they were closed, locked. The death-dart could not have come from outside the house. Horror gripped him as he searched the walls, seeking some possible secret aperture through which the murderer might have loosed his poisoned missile. But he found nothing—no spot from which the dart might have come.... And yet it had happened. Impossibly, fantastically, out of empty space, the dart had sped straight to Thora Gaxton's heart....

Horror and a sudden numbing fear bit into John Bryant's vitals as he launched himself headlong out of the library, ferreted through all the dark and empty rooms of the house. He found nothing, nobody. Then, at long last, he returned once more to the library—

And he was just in time to see the olive-skinned girl working at the fastenings of the bronze casket—trying to open its lid!

Bryant sprang at her, pinioned her. She struggled, tried to free herself. The heavy flannel dressing-gown, which Thora Gaxton had half-ripped from the girl's shoulders, now impeded her struggles. It had been torn open in front; and now her small breasts rose and fell sharply with her agonized, panting breath. "Let me go—let me go!" she cried.

Grimly Bryant held her, mashed her against him; and the nearness of her almost-nude body sent sudden thrills racing through his veins. He had an abrupt, atavistic desire to kiss her insanely; to clamp his lips savagely upon her mouth....

And then the sensation passed. Reason returned: He was once more cool, collected, grim. He stared into the girl's terrified dark eyes. "You didn't kill Thora Gaxton!" he said. "But her death is somehow connected with your presence in this house. Now—you're going to tell me!"

"No! *No!*" she wailed.

"Yes," he panted unevenly. "You're going to tell me *why you have gone three times to that bronze casket!*"

Fear-maggots slithered in her eyes. Suddenly she clung to him, fused and melted her lovely unclad body against him, so that he was filled with leaping desire for her. "You—you must not ask me!" she panted. "Just—let me go! Otherwise... it will mean—death—!"

"Death? For whom?"

"For you—and perhaps for me!" she cried out. Once again she clung to him. "You must believe me! I had nothing to do with—with the murder of your cousin's wife. I did not know—did not anticipate—" Then, suddenly, she was silent, obdurate even in the face of the inexplicable terror that gripped and held her in its tentacle thralls.

John Bryant knew sudden pity for her. And something of her fear communicated itself to the secret places of his soul. He gripped himself hard; fought for his courage. "Thora's death is connected with that bronze casket, isn't it?" he whispered.

The girl would not answer him; would not meet his eyes. Terror marred her lovely features; sent shudders through her form.

"I'm going to open the thing—see what's in it!" Bryant said grimly.

"No—no!" She clung to him, tried to stop him.

He held her wrists with his left hand; then, with his right, he unfastened the catches on the bronze casket's heavy lid—

"Don't touch that chest! If you do I'll kill you!" a voice snarled from the doorway of the library.

John Bryant whirled—and stared into the rage-distorted face of his cousin, Dr. William Gaxton!

The surgeon held an automatic in his right fist; and he was leveling its round black muzzle full at John Bryant's heart. He had entered silently, unobserved, undetected.

"Bill—Bill Gaxton! For God's sake!" John Bryant cried out. "What in heaven's name—"

For a split second, the surgeon's eyes licked toward the corpse of his wife on the floor. "You killed Thora! You and this South American slut!" he foamed insanely.

"You're mad!" John Bryant rasped.

"Enough! You're in league with those who seek to destroy me! You've sold out to those who want revenge! I'm going to kill you!" And the surgeon's finger tightened on the trigger of his blue-barreled automatic.

John Bryant steeled himself for the crashing impact of a leaden slug, for he read the murder-frenzy in his cousin's mad eyes. But before Gaxton could fire, something happened—

Something impossible, weird, unbelievable. Suddenly, Dr. Gaxton emitted a wild shriek. The automatic dropped from his hand. His long fingers went clawing toward his neck, above his collar. "God!" he gibbered. *"It's got me!"*

And then a greenish pallor spread swiftly over his face—the same putrescent hue that had marked Thora Gaxton's white features just before she had died. The surgeon swayed, staggered.

John Bryant choked out an oath. "What in hell's name—!" he gasped. He released his hold on the olive-skinned girl; sprang toward his cousin. But already the surgeon had fallen to the floor; was writhing horribly in the convulsions of a torturing death-agony.

Bryant flung himself down beside his stricken cousin—but he was too late; and he knew it ominously well. Already the surgeon's eyes were dilated, glassy, staring. His muscles were horribly rigid as some swift, toxic poison raced through his distended veins. Foam flecked his lips, and his tongue protruded thickly.... Abruptly he went limp, lifeless....

"Another poison-dart!" John Bryant gasped from his constricted throat. His gaze went to a tiny blood-globule on his cousin's neck, just over the jugular. In the center of that crimson globule there glittered a metallic pin-point of silver, deadly and venomous—

Nor could the dart have been sped on its murderous way by

He rolled her over. There was froth on her lips.

the olive-skinned girl; because John Bryant had been pinioning her in his arms when his cousin had fallen....

Bryant lurched to his feet. "By the living God—there's someone hiding in this very room!" he grated savagely. *"Someone with a blow-gun!"*

Intuitively, he lanced himself toward the corner where that casket-like bronze chest rested upon its funereal pedestal of black onyx.

The South American girl tried to stop him. He flung her aside with a sweeping blow of his open hand. She staggered and lost her footing; fell to the floor beside him. He gained the casket, wrenched at its fastenings—

"Dios—look out!" the girl cried wildly, frantically.

John Bryant ducked. He heard a faint, metallic ping against the bronze side of the casket—where his own hand had been a bare instant before. Something glittered and fell to the carpet. *Another poison dart!*

And it had missed John Bryant by a mere inch!

Bryant pivoted, stared. But there was nobody in the room with him except the olive-skinned girl and the dead corpses of Dr. Gaxton and Thora, at the other end of the library. Nobody else, except... the unseen killer....

Suddenly, from the divan, there arose a thin, mewling wail. The olive-skinned girl scrambled frantically to her feet. "I've got to get him out of here!" she gasped wildly. She raced toward the infant.

John Bryant leaped at her, caught her. "No!" he rasped. "Not until the storm's over and I can phone the police!"

Then he lifted the girl into his arms, sped out of the library. And even as he crossed the threshold, a blinding flash of lightning split the sky outside the house; and suddenly the electric lights flickered weirdly, blazed up—and died into utter darkness.... The darkness of the tomb....

In the outer hallway, John Bryant crouched, holding the girl so tightly in his grasp that she could not struggle, could not fight free of his encompassing arms. The heavy flannel robe hung about her lithe waist, fastened by its belt-cord; her upper torso was bared and sweetly nude. Now in the darkness, Bryant knew the damp fragrance of her hair in his nostrils, felt the palpitant firmness of her unclad, rounded breasts against him, feminine and alluring....

His lips crept close to her ear. "Be still!" he whispered. "It's our only chance! I've got to catch him unaware—!"

"Catch—who do you mean?" she panted swiftly.

"The murderer!" he answered.

He felt her silk-smooth muscles tighten and tense in his arms. She drew a sharp, agonized breath. In the utter blackness that surrounded them like a shroud, his hand sought her naked bosoms, cupped them gently. "I know the answer to the riddle!" he breathed into her ear.

"You—you have guessed...?"

"Yes!"

"Then—*Madonna mia*—you must think that I—"

He crushed her against him; and abruptly she clung to his stalwart form, merging and fusing her semi-nude body against his own. Her arms went helplessly about his neck, filling him with lancing tingles. "I believe in your innocence!" he told her in an ardent whisper.

"You must!" she shuddered. "I did not know that he intended to… murder…."

"Sh-h-h-!" John Bryant stiffened. "Listen!" And then he started to creep silently toward the door of the library.

Convulsively the girl clung to him, tried to stay him. "Do not go in there!" she panted. "He might—kill you!"

"Would it matter… to you?" She pressed against him; and in the darkness her lips came toward his mouth. His fingers traversed the smooth planes of her perfect back, the ripening contours of her breasts…. He tasted the dewy sweetness of her kiss… "I love you, John Bryant!" she whispered frantically. "I don't want you to die! Stay here with me!" Her whisper was importunate, desperate.

In that instant, the floodgates of John Bryant's passion were unlocked. He kissed the girl—kissed her eyes, her lips, the warm hollow of her throbbing, flawless throat. Reverently he brushed the satin skin of her breasts with his tingling finger-tips….

Then he gently pushed her away from him. "I'll be safe!" he promised. And he started once more for the door of the library.

As he gained the threshold, the dying flames on the room's hearth illumined the chamber with a weird, hell-red glow. Bryant stared through narrowed eyes—

A tiny, dim figure was clambering up that black onyx pedestal; was wrenching at the catches of the small bronze casket. The lid opened slowly. The tiny figure uttered a sharp, bitter cry.

And at that instant, John Bryant hurled himself forward into the room. His hurtling form smashed across the intervening space, plummeted against the onyx pedestal. It toppled, fell, shattered with a splintering crash that broke the silence like a dissonance from hell. And the bronze casket, which had rested atop the pedestal, struck heavily against the floor—and against something else… something soft and yielding.…

Its sharp corner impacted horribly upon the skull of that tiny figure which had crawled and clambered up the pedestal; landed with a nauseating, crunching sound, as of a huge egg-shell being smashed.…

With a sickened cry, John Bryant tugged at the heavy little casket, pulled it away. Then he stared downward; stared into the smashed, crunched features of a dead man—

A midget!

The midget who had been brought into this house of horror in the guise of a mewling infant!

The dwarf lay there in a widening pool of blood, his skull split wide open by the corner of the heavy bronze casket. Bryant saw the midget's swarthy face—and then he saw something else. In the dwarf's tiny right fist there was a short, murderous blow-gun!

"I thought so!" Bryant rasped thickly. "And now there's just one more question!" He bent over the bronze casket, opened it.…

His face suddenly drained of color.

There, in a satin-lined nest, was the exquisite, olive-ivory corpse of another midget.… A woman, tiny, perfectly-formed, utterly and exquisitely nude. Unutterably, unbelievably lovely was her face, framed in a halo of coal-dark, midnight hair. Poignantly beautiful was her tiny, doll-like body with its lilting, mature hips and its miniature, nubile breasts.…

John Bryant touched the lovely, satin-smooth skin. And then cold horror struck through his marrow, congealed the blood in his veins. "God in heaven!" he breathed.

From behind him, a feminine voice said, "Now… you can understand!"

John Bryant whirled, saw the South American girl. Her lips trembled as she spoke. "Your cousin, Dr. William Gaxton, attended that beautiful midget woman in Quito, two years ago. She suffered a minor ailment; but your cousin falsely diagnosed her illness, claimed that a major surgical operation was necessary. Deliberately he permitted her to die under his cruel scalpel…

because he wanted her body!"

"God!" John Bryant choked.

"By a stratagem, Dr. Gaxton gained possession of her corpse. He... used it to practice his hellish taxidermy. He stuffed that poor, innocent cadaver—mounted it—kept it as the supreme specimen of his skill! Brought it back to the United States with him when he retired from his practice in Ecuador!"

"And—and this other one? This other dwarf?" John Bryant pointed to that second tiny corpse on the floor—the miniature man who had been killed by the falling bronze casket.

"He was... my brother. And he was... the husband of the girl in that bronze casket!"

"Lord!" Bryant muttered.

"He learned that your cousin had permitted his tiny wife to die on the operating table, just in order to preserve her body. He knew that Dr. Gaxton's wife, Thora, had been a partner in the crime. And then—"

"And then you brought him here for revenge?"

The girl paled. "No—no!" she wailed bitterly. "I was innocent of any knowledge of... my brother's intention to do murder. My brother made me believe that he merely wanted to recover his wife's body, so that he could give it decent burial. That is why I consented to bring him here disguised as an infant. I thought the plan was only to gain entrance to this house and steal the body from its bronze casket. I—I did not know that my brother had a blow-gun; that he intended to kill Dr. Gaxton and Dr. Gaxton's wife. Had I known that he was seeking such... such horrible vengeance, I would not have brought him...."

The girl closed her eyes, swayed weakly. John Bryant leaped toward her, caught her in his arms. "My dear—my dear!" he whispered tenderly. "It's all right. I believe you. I know that you could not possibly have been involved in any murder plan. You are too sweet, too innocent, too lovely...."

"And you... forgive me?"

John Bryant looked toward the body of his dead cousin, Dr. William Gaxton; remembered that moment when the surgeon had burst into the library with an automatic.... Bryant knew, then, that Gaxton would have killed him, had not the midget's poison-dart intervened. Then it was that John Bryant realized the fullness of his cousin's warped insanity....

"It is probably better that Gaxton died!" Bryant whispered.

"And you can see the position I was placed in? You can understand why I dared not tell the truth, after Thora Gaxton had been murdered?" the girl whispered tremulously.

"Yes," John Bryant answered gravely. "You knew that your midget brother had turned maniac; had become a murderer. You knew that if you gave him away, he would kill you with his blow-gun!"

"It—it was not that," the girl confessed. "It was because I feared he might... kill you!"

John Bryant looked at her; read the mute appeal in her liquid eyes. And then he kissed her, with a tenderness that held promise of happiness to come.

JOHN BARD

ChE SECOND MUMMY

*For the thief who stole his mummies, the
old Cacique had a coffin. But no threat
could keep Ernie from the girl he loved.*

E*rnie Slade of* the Chicago firm of "Martin and Slade,
Detectives" surveyed the smashed glass front of the show-
case in the *Muséo Nacionál* with something akin to awe. This was
not only peculiar, it was unnatural.

"Seven nights in a row, huh?" he said to his old friend, the
curator.

"Exactamente," admitted Dr. José Sandoval. "Ernie, it is the
mos' strange thing. All the nights since I have remove her from
the museum safe and place her in the display case it has happen.
Each day I have the caretaker replace the glass. Each morning it
is break... and yet she is still there, my beautiful Ixtaxihuatl, she
has not been rob...."

"Ixtaxihuatl?" said Ernie, puzzled, looking closely at the perfect
little figurine in the doctor's withered brown hand. The name, or
was it the figure? stirred some distant memory.

"That is her name. In your admirable *Inglés* it mean, 'The White
Woman.' She is the mos' precious possession of the *Muséo Nacionál.* I rob her myself from a *Cacique* in the market in Chiapas."

Ernie laughed heartily at this bit of engaging frankness as he
carefully took the figurine from the doctor's outstretched hand.
It was not more than ten inches high. The obsidian-colored hair

70

was braided in a coronet around the doll-like head. The face, with closed eyes, and finely chiseled nose and mouth was as smooth as carven ivory. The slender neck arose queen-like from pale onyx shoulders. Ernie's eyes opened a little as they reached the breasts, milky-white mounds moulded with such perfection that he felt his pulse quicken in spite of himself. He could not resist touching the tiny body with his finger. It felt warm, almost human. The blood in his finger began to hammer. He closed his eyes momentarily. Was it his pulse that hammered? He opened his eyes, bewildered.

Below the full breasts the delicately curved stomach was so natural it seemed to have been caught in the midst of a breath and petrified by some strange instantaneous process. The youthful hips and seductively curved waist were partially hidden by a girdle of precious stones. The slender shapely legs ended in tiny bare feet.

"Whew," said Ernie, licking his lips. "I don't blame you for stealing her. She gives me a yen just to look at her. But I can't believe this little doll was once a life-sized girl, José."

"Es verdad! Seguramente! I know is so. Is not the first time I have see a doll-mummy. But is the first I have ever possess. The art of concentrated mummification is lost. It is know only by this very old *Cacique* and he will not give or sell it. With him it will die. Is for that reason I valuable Ixtaxihuatl so much. Is for that reason I rob her from him. But the *Cacique* is a *Mago.* He is know all the ancient *brujeriá,* the witchcraft of his tribe. Now he send, I am sure, a *demonio* through barred windows and locked doors to plague me, to rob back his *momía-muñeca,* his doll-mummy."

Ernie laughed, "So you think the old chief has sent a demon to persecute you. Well, José, tell me this. If this demon can come in through locked doors and break the glass on the front of the show-case, why can't he take Ixtaxihuatl and go out through the same locked doors? Why does he break the glass without removing the mummy?"

The doctor shrugged his thin shoulders. *"Quien sabe?* But last night I speak to myself. I say, 'I lie myself a trap.' I sprinkle white powder on the floor before the case. *Mira!* Look what I have

"No! No!" she cried. "If you kill, we cannot love!"

catch! Feetprints!"

Ernie followed the doctor's pointing finger. On the red tile floor very close to the edge of the display case three naked footprints were etched in the white powder. They were small, not much larger than a child's. Ernie's practiced eyes narrowed critically. An eyebrow elevated interrogatively. He whistled.

"*Qué pasa?*" asked the doctor.

"*Nada.* Nothing at all, except if I stood in front of a glass case to break it, my footprints would face the case, not lead away from it. And it is customary for shattered glass to fall away from the blow, not toward it. The majority of the broken glass should be inside the case, not outside on the floor."

"So?" said the doctor, slightly puzzled.

Ernie leaned closer to the footprint on his left. Very carefully

he picked up a triangular sliver of glass. He held it up in a ray of the morning sun that came in through one of the tall windows. One sharp edge was darkened by a stain.

"Let's have another squint at Ixtaxihuatl, Joe."

The doctor passed him the figurine once more. In a half joking manner as if he were speaking to the figurine he said, "I hate to do this to a lady." Then he stood Ixtaxihuatl on her head in the palm of his hand. He was amazed to see how life-like was every curve of her tiny body. He examined closely the bottoms of her feet. On the ball of the right foot was a tiny scratch and a very small spot of brown stain.

Ernie whistled again very softly.

"José *amigo,*" he said, ticking his tongue sibilantly against his teeth, "you're a venerable, heartless, wicked old wretch. I come two thousand miles to Mexico on a vacation and, because you couldn't resist the physical charms of this Chiapas maiden, I have to get back on the job." He handed Ixtaxihuatl, with a kind of gentle tenderness, back to the doctor. "Tell me, José, what do you know about *suspended animation?*"

The doctor, startled at this irrelevant question, hesitated a moment. "*Pues,*" he began rhetorically, "suspended animation is the practice of a Hindu. Is condition of the body brought about by mental...."

"Isn't it," interrupted Ernie, "a halting of the functions of the body without death? A sort of... immortality?"

The doctor pondered a moment, "*Pues,* one may call it that."

"Have the caretaker replace the glass again, José, and put the lovely maiden back in her case. I've got an idea. By the way, you haven't got one of those boards filled with spikes that the Hindus sit on, to torture themselves?"

"*Como no?* Is in the Asiatic section. I will show it to you."

"I don't want to see it," laughed Ernie. "I want to sit on it tonight to keep me awake."

The sarcophagus stank. The stench of musty age and rotting wood. The lid was off so that Ernie might jump out quickly if necessary, but it wasn't pleasant lying in a mummy coffin when the mummy had only been removed five hours before. It had been his idea to lie in wait like this for the *Thing* that made footprints backward, made broken glass defy natural laws, and apparently passed unaided through locked doors and barred windows.

The grandfather clock in the American section had finally bonged the hour of ten and Ernie was beginning to think it would have been better if he'd stuck to his original suggestion of the torture seat. He was constantly nodding. His feet had gone to sleep. His nether region was number from sitting. His spine prickled continuously. A spot on his thigh burned steadily from the pressure of the ring of museum keys that Sandoval had given him.

But his eyes, when they were open, never left the glass case that the rays of the moon were just beginning to reach.

The moon climbed higher, finally engulfing the square, glass case in a pale silver glow that accentuated the blackness of the velvet on which the little *momía-muñeca* lay. Ernie's head drooped once more upon his chest. He slept.

He was awakened instantly by a crash of broken glass. His head jerked up. His eyes glued to the front of the show-case where a great jagged hole had been torn in the glass. Against the background of black velvet he saw something move. His hand went to his shoulder holster. A head appeared through the hole in the show-case. Ernie stared. He shook his head vaguely. Where had he seen that face before?

The hair, black as obsidian, was braided in a coronet around her head. The finely chiseled nose and mouth were in a face like carven ivory. Pale onyx shoulders followed the lovely head. Full, pearl-like breasts, touched with silver by the bright moon, swayed gently to the graceful movement of her curved white thighs as she stepped mincingly to avoid the broken glass on the floor. Around her youthful, luscious hips a jeweled girdle flashing red, green, blue, and white hid just enough of the delicious figure to make Ernie suck in his breath.

Without moving, Ernie watched her pass within three feet of his hiding place, saw the intent look of her brown eyes, the queenly poise of her slender neck, the gentle bobbing of her ripe young breasts. He could feel the eager thumping of his heart, the pleasant tightening of his muscles. Quietly he got to his feet.

Then he saw it!

In her pale white hand she carried the *momía-muñeca!* Stepping from the sarcophagus he followed her noiselessly on his rubber-soled shoes. She went from door to door, trying each knob vigorously and each time venting little whimpering cries like a very young puppy that has been left alone. At each of the great windows she stopped, her almost naked body a luscious silhouette, and looked helplessly at the great iron bars that cut off the way to freedom. At last, with a graceful little shrug of despair she turned back to retrace her steps.

Ernie was waiting in the shadow beside the window. With a swift movement he grabbed the *momía-muñeca* from her tiny

"Give me my body!" she cried. "Give me my body!"

hand and leaped into the square of moonlight in front of the window.

She followed him instantly with a shrill little cry of dismay. Her words were of a strange tongue but, as if words were unessential, their meaning flashed clear in his mind.

"Give me my body," she was crying. "Give me my body!"

He placed the doll-mummy on the ledge of the window behind him so that it would not be broken and, standing directly in front of it, met the onslaught of the tigress that leaped upon him.

She was not large, not more than five feet tall, but she fought as if it meant her very life to regain that doll-like image. In silence she bit, she gouged, she clawed his face until he felt the hot blood dripping. She fastened her teeth into his wrist until he almost cried out with the pain. He drew her hot, panting body against him, crushing her until she seemed to scorch him through his shirt.

He pulled her arms behind her and, locking them with one hand, he clutched with the other her coiled obsidian hair and jerked back her head. Then, he planted his mouth brutally across her flower-like lips drinking in her breath until it seemed she must suffocate.

Gradually her struggling subsided. Her gently heaving breasts quivered docilely against him. Her whole body seemed to shiver with a sort of ecstasy. A pleasant woman-scent assailed his nostrils. His head floated. His whole body trembled with a kind of delightful ague. He seemed to grow in height. His muscles swelled. He was engulfed in a stabbing, joyous delirium....

It was a long time before she spoke again in that strange tongue that he seemed to understand without thinking. The words appeared like a photograph in his brain.

"Great Brute," she said, "I love you. You will not remember but I have always loved you. I loved you when you rode into my village with Cortez and Bernal Diaz and took me captive. I almost died when you were killed. It was my father who saved my life. He was the greatest of the *Magos*. He said, 'My daughter, you shall live to love again.' He drew a circle around me with the twig of life. And I lived. I loved you when you were Hacendado of our land. It was my hand that nursed you when you died of plague. I should have died of grief then had I not been bound to life. I love you now, foreigner, though I did not know you till you touched me, till you struck the spark of love into my heart. Tell me that you love me, too. Even though you lie...."

It was Ernie's burning lips that drowned her words. He kissed her until she almost swooned, drawing in the perfume of her lungs, becoming one with her. There was no one else, just they two. They had left the world behind.

He drew his wet lips away and whispered husky words between each gentle kiss. "I... do... love... you... Ixtaxihuatl...."

The demand came to his brain again. "Then give me back my body. Without it I cannot live till *then*...."

"*Then...?*"

"Till the final *then* when you and I are one."

In a sort of brilliant daze Ernie Slade picked up the doll-mummy from the window ledge and pressed it in her hand.

He heard himself say, "Here is your body, Ixtaxihuatl, but if you take it away from me, I shall come for it again."

Ernie *saw* her last words clearly. "You *shall* come for my body again. That is your destiny." The brilliance in the room died out and there was nothing. Only blackness.

The funny noise that Ernie heard as he slowly regained consciousness was the voice of his friend, Dr. Sandoval. The doctor was talking to someone else. He was saying, "The keys they had been take from his pocket. I find them in the open door. Unfortunately the *momía-muñeca* has been rob. It is the only one. I cannot replace it."

Ernie sat up slowly, "I can, José," he said.

What was that brilliant light that hovered in his brain? The sun, of course; it was morning. But he could *see* the words there in the light. He could hear that silent voice.

He said, "José, is there a place called Nopalcingo?"

"*Sí, amigo mío*. In Chiapas north of Guatemala. It was near there at the market of Tlacalo that I find Ixtaxihuatl...."

"It is there, then, I will find her...."

The plane arrived at dawn the next morning. They landed in a field, vivid yellow with *Flores de la Muerte*, flowers of death. Ernie leaped down and started for the little group of mud-plastered bamboo *jacales*. He could see the conical roofs of *jalapa*, split palm fronds, over the rise of ground. The pilot could have landed nearer to the village, but he was superstitious. He had said, "It is the town of walking dead."

But Ernie Slade was above superstition. He shouted over his shoulder as he walked, "Cut your motor and save gas, I won't be long." He had just reached the top of the rise and could look down on the little hollow where the *pueblacita* nestled, calm and sleepy in the morning sun when he heard the roar of the plane's motor and saw the yellow heads of the *Flores de la Muerte* bend flat beneath the wind. The pilot waved an ironical farewell, as he gunned steadily to gain height for the mountain range behind him.

"What a sap I was," said Ernie, "to pay him in advance."

With a shrug he turned his back upon the receding plane. Resentment could find no place within him because his body smouldered with a greater emotion. He was in love, deeply, passionately in love for the first time in his life. He had come to find Ixtaxihuatl and even though he had come by plane and she had been near-naked and on foot he was sure he would find her here. He hurried down the little knoll toward the group of dwellings in the hollow.

Then for the first time he saw the narrow black line that, python-like, completely encircled the little group of *jacales*. It was as if someone had taken crude oil and drawn a circle within which were the confines of the village, beyond which was the free and open country. He approached it with a peculiar feeling of suspense. Only then it occurred to him how odd it was that no dogs barked their incessant challenge. Chickens scrabbling in the dust, goats plucking the withered grass, did not even turn their heads as he approached. It was as if they did not see him.

He reached the curving black line. It was about three inches wide and gave the impression of being not only on the surface of the ground but to have depth. He bent forward to examine it more closely. The top of his head came into such violent contact with some hard substance that he found himself suddenly lying flat on his back.

He got up, mystified, rubbing the bump that was quickly forming on the top of his head. It was then that the dogs began to bark, that the chickens and goats looked up at this commotion. Even a few natives in dirty white *calzones, camisas,* and *faldas* appeared at the door-less openings of the mud *jacales*. One old Indian, creased and shriveled like an apple that has dried in the sun, started walking forward.

Taking that for a good omen, Ernie started across the black line. He stopped more suddenly than he began. It was as if he walked full on into a stone wall. His nose flattened painfully. His forehead began to ache from the blow it received. His knees were bruised from contact with this unseen something that he could not penetrate.

While Ernie tentatively felt of his nose to see if it were broken, the old Indian approached the other side of the black line. He walked as if he did not even see Ernie, as if there were a wall-like haze his old eyes could not penetrate. He reached a point opposite the spot where Slade was standing. His scrawny, skeleton-like hand went out and threw back an invisible latch. Ernie could hear the metallic click. Then the hand took hold of an unseen door knob and seemed to open a door because Ernie could feel a cool breeze come through the doorway. The old Indian beckoned.

Very hesitantly Slade edged forward. He was in a sort of daze. He tried to think that all this hokus-pokus was perfectly proper, that he *had* bumped into an invisible wall, that he was stepping through a doorway he couldn't see, but he was convinced that he was still lying on the floor of the *Muséo Nacionál* and this was a cock-eyed dream.

He followed the withered old Indian, each step making a nimbus of dust around his feet. The dogs came out and barked as he passed each *jacal*. The sloe-eyed natives gazed at him passively. No greetings were made, no inclinations of the head, no demonstrations. Not a word was spoken. There seemed to be no need of any. The old Indian knew where Ernie wanted to go and Ernie knew the old Indian was taking him there.

Ahead of them in the dusty space that passed for a street was a round stone basin, a *fuente*. Water poured from over its smooth sides, forming a tiny stream that flowed between the houses. Sitting in the basin soberly washing her lovely body was a white-skinned girl. She lifted water in a *jicora*, half of a gourd, and poured it over her face and breast. Ernie stopped in his tracks at the sight. His heart leaped within him. His blood raced. He shouted.

"*Ixtaxihuatl...!*"

The girl stood up instantly. In one hand she held the *jicora*, in the other the sparkling jeweled girdle. In the instant that she stood there, naked, looking at him Ernie recognized all the lovely curves of her luscious body. The full-blown, new ivory breasts, the youthful delicately carved hips, the grace of her whole posture.

Then, fleet as a deer, she leaped from the *fuente* and sped toward a large *jacal* that towered above the others because it was on stilts. With admiration Ernie watched the swift, graceful movement of her thighs as she climbed the rough-made ladder. With his eyes he kissed her blood-red, parted lips. He was entranced.

Then suddenly he realized he was alone. The old Indian was gone. But now he knew the house. Walking rapidly he stepped across the little stream from the fountain and came to the foot of the ladder. He hesitated, would have rapped or spoken, but he *saw* the sweet voice in his brain. It said, "Come up, beloved!"

As rapidly as he could climb with safety, he reached the little platform-like porch in front of the door. There he hesitated once more. Through the doorway came the most ancient, wrinkled, nut-brown *Cacique* that he had ever seen. He looked as if he might be old as the earth itself. Ernie knew he was *Cacique* by the leather band around his forehead. The old chief stood aside and motioned him to enter. He spoke four words in Spanish, "My house is yours."

Ernie felt it best to state his business. "I come, *Venerable Cacique,* to ask for the hand of your daughter."

"I have no daughter."

"Then, your niece."

"I have no niece."

"Then, the lovely girl who is in your house."

"There is no girl in my house. Will you enter, friend?"

Ernie, puzzled by this denial, passed from the bright sunlight into the cool darkness of the little room. He looked vainly for the white form of Ixtaxihuatl. The room was empty. There were no chairs. Only *petates,* palm mats, upon the floor. In one corner was a carved stone *brasera* for charcoal. Sitting along the floor against the woven bamboo wall were cooking utensils, *ollas, casuelas, ollitas,* and a large flat *comal* of red clay for baking *tortillas.* There were black *loza* bowls for drinking and a *jicora* for dipping water. Ernie noticed that the *jicora* was wet.

Then for the first time Ernie saw, beyond the *brasera,* a small doorway. He inclined his head in that direction and said, *"Permiso?"*

The *Cacique* with a grave smile gave permission. The doorway gave onto a back porch covered by a slanting roof of *palapa.* It was empty. Feeling sheepish, puzzled, and defeated Ernie once more entered the little room. From this new angle he saw to the left of the front doorway a small Spanish chest with an ancient

curved top, bound by carven bronze bands, the wood inlaid with obsidian and mother of pearl. The *chapo*, a hand hammered lock of bronze, was beautiful and very strong. He could have sworn the chest was not there when he had entered.

"You admire my *cajón*," said the *Cacique*. "Would you like to see its contents?"

"If it is your pleasure, *Cacique*."

"*Miramos*," said the *Cacique*, bending down to unlock it and pushing back the lid.

Inside the *cajón* were five *cajonitas*, smaller chests of rosewood but very plain. The old *Cacique* lifted the lid of the first one. It was lined with deer skin. On the soft leather lay a peculiar x-shaped piece of round wood. Two branches seemed to have crossed and grown together.

"The twig of life," said the *Cacique*. "Look well. No strange eyes have seen these things before."

Ernie felt an odd contraction around his heart as if his stomach had risen to devour it. "Then why do you show them to me?"

The *Cacique* opened the lid of the second box and looked at Ernie with eyes of great depth. "*You* have been chosen," he said.

Slade felt his stomach sink back into place as he looked at the contents of the second box. It was filled with a heavy, lustrous black liquid. Ernie thought of the circular black line.

"The impenetrable oil," said the *Cacique.*

A third chest was opened. It was listed with thin hammered gold, and filled to the top with a colorless sparkling liquid.

"The oil of concentration," said the *Cacique.* And Ernie thought of the *momía-muñeca,* his beautiful Ixtaxihuatl.

Ernie watched breathlessly while the old *Cacique* opened the fourth chest. Surely this must contain…. No. It was empty. He looked once more to make sure.

He said, "Is there

Ernie saw her… his blood raced. He shouted: "Ixtaxihuatl!"

something there I cannot see?"

"There is nothing there," said the *Cacique* closing the lid, "yet."

The fifth chest was open. In it lay the lovely white figure of the *momía-muñeca,* Ixtaxihuatl. Her beauty drowned him in a wave of ecstasy.

He said huskily, "I love her. Let me take her with me."

"She cannot leave."

"I love her. Let me buy her."

"She is not for sale."

Ernie, tortured by the old man's calm refusal, drew the automatic from his shoulder holster and whirled upon him.

"Then I will *take* her!"

There was a little scream of dismay and Ernie suddenly found Ixtaxihuatl, with the *momía-muñeca* in one hand, standing between himself and the ancient *Cacique.*

"No, no," she cried. "You must not kill. I love you. You are my man. I want you to live till *then.* If you take life, you cannot live. That is the law."

Ernie found himself smothered in her embrace. Her body panted against his. He dropped the pistol to the *petate* covered floor and clasped his arms around her warm body. He could feel her breasts, round and burning, against his chest. Her lips fastened over his with such intensity that she seemed to draw the very blood from his brain. He was dazed by a flood of thrills. His whole being throbbed to the heat of her enveloping body. He was consumed in one great white flame of ecstasy.

In the market place at Tlacalo, ten kilometros by burro from Nopalcingo, sat the most ancient, wrinkled, nut-brown *Cacique* that you could hope to see. He looked as if he might be old as the earth itself. You knew he was *Cacique* by the leather band around his head. On a *petate* in front of him, arranged in neat little *montones,* were thirty different kinds of yerbas, herbs for healing. At his side were three tiny rosewood chests.

Dr. José Sandoval, curator of the *Muséo Nationál,* approached the old Cacique with an odd mixture of reverence and fear. He stopped in front of the *petate* with the thirty different kinds of herbs, and took his wallet from his pocket.

"*Compra yerbas?*" asked the old *Cacique*.

"No," said the doctor in Spanish. "I want to pay you for the *momía-muñeca*. I cannot return it. It has been stolen from me. How much do you want?"

"Nothing, señor doctor. I have the *momia-muneca*. I am its guardian. It always comes back to me. Would you like to see it once more?"

"Yes," breathed the doctor, "I would."

The old *Cacique* picked up one of the rosewood chests and lifted the lid. In it lay what appeared to Dr. Sandoval to be the most beautiful thing in the world... Ixtaxihuatl.

"I would give my soul to have her," said the doctor simply.

"A fair exchange, but she has been claimed by another."

Then the doctor said what he had really come all this distance to say. "I have come, *Venerable Cacique,* to look for my friend, Ernie Slade. He is *Americano....*"

The old Cacique, without seeming to listen, was opening the second chest. He held it out for the doctor to see. In it lay a *momía-muñeca,* white as Ixtaxihuatl and as perfectly formed but in a different way. This doll-mummy was a man.

The doctor, speechless, with a terrible feeling of nausea at the pit of his stomach looked at the mummy's tiny face. It must be.... It had to be.... It was... his friend.

The old *Cacique* was calmly holding out the third rosewood chest. In spite of himself the doctor looked inside. It was empty. The doctor quivered with a kind of ague.

"This chest," the old *Cacique* said mildly, "is for the thief who steals my mummies."

Dr. José Sandoval was an old man, but he was able to run. He ran.

JUSTIN CASE

MISTRESS OF VENGEANCE

*Seven men came back, leaving thirty
behind. And behind that fact was only
the perfume of a jungle flower and the
fatal beauty of weird, lovely women!*

There were seven of us, and for want of a better name we called ourselves The Ancients. We weren't ancient, of course, but of the thirty-seven who began that terrifying journey into the South American wilds, we were the only ones who returned. Seven out of thirty-seven! And tonight, impatiently awaiting the arrival of my companions, I was alone in the gloomy Cape Cod house which had been my home for three dreary months.

I was alone, yet staring intently into the face of a woman!

She had come silently out of some dark, adjoining chamber and was standing now within arm's reach of me, just beyond the glow cast by the lamp which reared its ugly, antique head behind my chair. Something about her was vaguely sinister. I stared at her, yet feared to lean forward and touch her.

God, she was lovely! Raven black hair framed the amazing whiteness of her face. Her lips formed a scarlet-rimmed well of mystery which I wanted madly to explore. Her arms undulated toward me and remained outstretched. Her exotic beauty sent flame-headed spiders of desire racing through my veins!

She wore no clothes, no civilized garb of any kind—only a thin, web-like girdle fashioned from the skin of some tropical animal, a skin as thin, as delicate, as the fibrous tissue between the toes of a bat. Every sinuous carve of her ivory-hued body was revealed to my avid gaze, and every curve seemed to be vibrantly alive, passionately begging the embrace of my aching arms.

I slid slowly forward in my chair, stopped, fell back again, knowing somehow that I was in the fearsome presence of a thing more dangerous than death itself. Something about this exotic woman of the night was hellishly familiar! Somewhere, long ago, I had seen other men yield to the allure of her sinuous beauty, and they had died horribly, screaming out their agonies while those red lips laughed softly in evil triumph....

Somewhere, too, I had been warned against the drug-like perfume which seemed to be emanating now from those same carmine lips, and from the lilting mounds of her ivory breasts, and from the jet glory of her hair. That heady fragrance was treacherous. It lured men to their doom!

I knew then that she was one of the hell-born creatures we had encountered three years ago, on that night of jungle inferno when men had gone mad with fear. She had come for me....

My blood, which a moment ago had burned hot, became suddenly cold as liquid air. Terror numbed me. "Go back," I muttered. "Go back where you came from!" And I heard low, liquid laughter as the woman retreated slowly into enveloping darkness.

She was gone! I blinked my eyes, listened a moment to the fearsome din of the storm outside. Gone! Good Lord, had I been *dreaming?* A fire was blazing in the big parlor furnace; the lamp behind my chair threw yellow shadows over the worn carpet. All around me the old house was creaking and groaning in the teeth of the wind, while gusts of rain sledged furiously at the windows.

Dreaming? I laughed nervously, and pushed myself erect as the shrill blast of an automobile horn came eerily from the road outside. The laughter died in my throat. I stood still, pulled air into my lungs and caught something much stronger, more fragrant, than the usual reek of stale tobacco fumes. That exotic perfume again....

"No, it wasn't a dream," I muttered.

Lannister and the others misinterpreted the pallor of my face

as they came trooping in on me. Lannister, tall and husky, gazed about him, snorted, and said thickly: "Don't wonder you look sick, Dykes. This place is as cold as a morgue. What on earth possessed you to buy a house as old and as isolated as this?"

I didn't bother answering him. I had bought this place three months ago because it had seemed to offer the seclusion I needed for finishing a five-hundred page tome on our discoveries in South America. The house had formerly been occupied by an old man and his wife who were considered queer.

The woman died. Her husband, refusing to live here, rented the place to a nurse who came to Wellfield on a case. The nurse lived here just three weeks, then disappeared. The old man had seemed glad enough, after that, to sell the house to me and be rid of it.

I stared at my guests. Lannister had brought his daughter,

Hilda, a dark-haired, full-bosomed, glamorous girl of about twenty-two, who kept glancing at me over her cocktail glass. Young Trent had brought along his wife, Maryata, and I marveled at the fact that this savage jungle creature had acquired so much poise and polish during the three years she had been away from her jungle habitat.

Jones, Curtin, and Plummer had come alone. McClegg was missing.

"Where's McClegg?" I said.

They didn't know. They hadn't seen him or heard from him, any of them, in more than a month.

"Well," I said, "I'll tell you why I sent for you. It's really very simple. I've made enough money on magazine and newspaper articles, and in advance royalties on my book, to finance a second expedition. I want to go back there."

No one answered me. The gaze of every eye was focused unblinkingly upon me and the room was suddenly very still, except for the crackle of the fire and the din of the storm outside. I smiled grimly. It wasn't the first time a return trip to the jungle had been mentioned, nor was it the first time that dark memories had rushed in upon us and produced a silence born of fear.

That first expedition had been an affair of horror. Thirty-seven men had started the fateful journey. Most of the thirty-seven, led by Mark Lannister, had penetrated deep into uncharted regions south of the Oganoco. We had unearthed signs of a dead civilization. We had encountered a race of strangely alluring women who threatened us with death if we did not depart.

We defied the women. We violated the ruins of the dead city. Then a very strange, mind-eating disease attacked us. Some went mad, some died, others simply vanished and were not seen again. Disorganized, we fled from that region of hell and fought our way north to the Amazon.

Only seven of us endured the final horrors of that fearsome journey. On the way, young Trent met his Maryata—found her, a beautiful native girl, in a squalid village where we were looked upon as gods. For a handful of gold coins he bought her, took her with him. He married her when we reached the States.

Now I was talking of going back there!

"*It* will be dangerous," Lannister muttered. "I'm no coward, Dykes, but the thought terrifies me."

It terrified all of them, with the possible exception of the two women. Neither woman spoke, but both stared at me with an intensity that warmed my blood. I have a weakness for the admiration of beautiful women....

"I'll tell you my plans," I said, peering at Lannister.

I told them I had made arrangements to charter a freighter. I brought maps from another room and spread them on the floor. But I was treading on thin ice, and I knew it.

Terror was an unseen spectre among us. Terror was sapping the color from the faces I stared into, and was making brave men jump nervously at every alien noise produced by the storm. This old, gloomy house was partially responsible, I suppose; and I think some of the men were aware of the strange odor which seemed to be steadily growing stronger in the room. My talk of a return trip to the jungle was calling up memories which stretched every nerve to the breaking point.

Then it happened.

Young Trent, leaning forward in his chair to stare at one of the maps, suddenly stiffened, jerked his two hands up and began clawing at his throat! His face became white as chalk. Froth bubbled from the corners of his twitching mouth, and his eyes swelled horribly in their sockets.

He staggered erect, began screaming in a high, shrill voice that iced every drop of blood in my body. Then, wildly, he began laughing.

"It's the flowers!" he screamed. "The flowers that grew in the ruins of that damned city in the jungle! I'd know that smell anywhere! It drives men mad!"

Fate must have pointed a bloody forefinger in the direction of Hilda Lannister, for Trent singled her out and stumbled toward her, shrieking curses. "You're the cause of it!" he snarled. "You brought the flowers here to destroy us!" His left hand had swept out and snatched up the iron poker which leaned there against the stove.

Lannister and I got in front of him. It was Lannister, not I, who struck him—and Lannister had two hundred pounds of solid muscle to put behind the blow. I heard the fist grind into Trent's face. I heard bones crack.

The poker slid from Trent's hand. He spun slowly on one foot, slid to his knees and fell over backward. His head struck the iron base of the stove.

He was dead when Jones and Curtin and I carried him into the adjoining room. We worked over him in vain. When we closed the door and returned to our companions, Lannister was staring down at his clenched fist and moaning piteously, like a child who had done some terrible misdeed.

Trent's wife, Maryata, sat utterly motionless, staring into the fire. She didn't move, didn't speak. She seemed not to hear the shrill words that came pouring from the rest of us and turned the room into a place of bedlam.

Then we subsided, stared at her and realized the anguish that must be eating her heart out. She and Trent had loved each other. Trent was gone now—dead. Hilda Lannister went to Maryata's side and tried to console her.

Jones said grimly: "By God, there is an odor in this room! It's

At the foot of the ladder was a corpse! Terror came at me in a wave, paralyzing me.

time we found the cause of it!"

We searched the house. It took us a long time, and we left Lannister and Hilda to take care of Trent's stricken wife. Lannister wouldn't have been able to aid us, anyway; he was completely broken up by the hideous thing that had happened.

We separated, searched every room, found nothing. I met Jones on the stairs as he was descending from the musty chambers at the top of the house. He shook his head, stared at me. "The odor seems to be strongest in the living-room," he said.

When we reentered the living-room, the room was empty. I wondered dully where the Lannisters and Maryata Trent had gone to. Jones began sniffing like a bloodhound and presently dropped to his hands and knees, began crawling over the worn carpet.

Plummer and Curtin came into the room. Jones stopped crawling. "Come here, will you?" he said hoarsely, staring at me.

I strode toward him and knew that he had found something. He was close to the wall where Trent had been sitting. The exotic, drug-like odor was so strong where he knelt that it seemed to be a tangible, gaseous substance rising from the floor.

"Get a hammer and screw-driver," Jones said.

We pried up the floor-boards. When the job was done, I stood there, staring down in amazement at a black pit that extended into Stygian gloom at my feet. A crude wooden ladder slanted down into it.

"You knew this was here?" Plummer said, scowling at me.

I shook my head. "The house has no cellar," I said. "This is some secret crypt..."

They seemed to think it was my duty to descend first, so I went slowly down the ladder, taking a searchlight with me in one trembling fist. The pit was deep. When I got to the bottom, my head was a foot below floor-level. The searchlight's glare revealed a crypt about four feet square with earthen walls and floor. The air was hot, damp, and sickly sweet with the heady perfume which had driven Trent mad.

A thick-stemmed vine grew along one wall and reached half

a hundred snakelike tendrils toward the opening above. Its roots were imbedded in the soil at my feet. I stared at it and felt my eyes widening with horror. Small white flowers, cup-shaped and ambrosial, bloomed in profusion among its gnarled tentacles. Nowhere, *except amid the ruins of that ancient city in the jungles of South America,* had I seen its counterpart!

I kept away from it, fearing to touch it. Men had gone mad handling those exquisite blooms, or inhaling that aromatic scent! Behind me, Jones was groping his way down the ladder, and I moved aside to give him room. Then I saw the *other* thing.

It was a corpse.

Terror came at me in a gelid wave, paralyzing me. My blood ran cold. Jones said hoarsely, "God!" and leaned forward to peer into the corpse's countenance. Decay had already made it black and horrible.

"It's McClegg," Jones now muttered. "McClegg…. No wonder we haven't heard from him…." Then he wiped beads of sweat from his forehead and looked at me. "These flowers don't belong here. They don't grow anywhere in the United States. They've been planted here."

We had to go up before Plummer and Curtin could descend into the crypt. There wasn't room enough for all four of us. When the others rejoined us in the living-room, we talked the thing over and knew what we had to do. The corpse had to be taken out of there and disposed of. The vine must be ripped up by the roots and burned.

It took us a long time, and while we were at it, Maryata came into the room. She had been out in the storm. We stopped what we were doing and stared at her.

Evidently the death of her husband had done something to her mind. She had removed her shoes, most of her clothes, and unbound her hair, which was long and thick and hung now in a wet, gleaming mass, partially concealing the ivory mounds of her exquisite breasts. I thought for a moment that she was totally nude, until I saw the wet band of silk that encircled her enticing thighs.

Good Lord, had the death of young Trent shocked her into reverting to her former mode of living? Was she once more, at heart, a near-naked creature of the jungle?

I strode toward her. "Maryata," I said. "For God's sake, what are you doing? You mustn't—" But she ignored me. Gazing at all of us for an instant, as if wondering who we were and what we were doing, she walked quietly into the adjoining room and was gone.

I shook my head. "Poor girl," I muttered. "She's dazed by what happened." But our task was still unfinished, and I noticed that Plummer, who had insisted on doing the bulk of the work, was beginning to act queerly.

What time it was when we at last replaced the floor-boards over that black crypt, I don't know. I nailed the boards myself. When I straightened, Jones and Curtin were outside in the storm, disposing of the corpse. Plummer was standing beside the big parlor furnace, where the flames were devouring what was left of the strange vine which we had uprooted. The furnace door was open.

"You'd better close that," I said. "The odor from those burning blossoms may be—"

I didn't finish. Plummer's big body had suddenly begun to tremble violently. His back was toward me, so I couldn't see his face, but I saw him lurch forward, saw him plunge his right hand straight into the flames! The man had suddenly gone mad!

I tried to stop him, but the horrible thing was over before I even reached him. He wanted the flowers. If that crimson aperture in the furnace had been larger, he would have hurled his whole body through it; as it was, he buried his right arm to the elbow in red coals and then began screaming. I'll hear those horrible screams of torment in my sleep until death brings me a merciful release.

I lurched forward, yelling at him, but the room was full of his own lurid voice and he didn't hear me. He staggered back from the furnace, holding one end of the blazing vine in a black, twisted stump of hand that had been burned to the bone. He crushed the burning tentacles to his face and held them there with both hands, and then began laughing. *Laughing!* God!

Then agony seized him. He dropped the vine. He stared down at his mutilated arm, uttered a single blood-chilling scream and seized the sides of the furnace. When I got to him at last, he was beating his head frenziedly against the furnace door. He collapsed in my arms.

He died before I could get help.

I don't remember much of what happened after that. I was stunned, dazed. Lannister and Hilda came into the room, I think, and Hilda said she had taken her father out for a long walk in the storm, to calm him. I kept staring down at Plummer's bloody skull and at his charred hands. Maryata came wandering into the room, near-naked as before, and went out again, silently, after gazing for a moment at the corpse. Jones and Curtin returned and I told them what had happened.

It was Curtin who suggested that we all try to get some sleep. "The flowers were responsible for all this," he said, "and the flowers are burned now, so we have nothing more to be afraid of. In the morning we can all get out of here."

I went to my own room and closed the door. If there had been a key in the ancient lock, I would have locked myself in, but there wasn't. Without undressing I threw myself on the bed, leaving a lamp burning on the table.

I remember hearing a clock strike three. Three A.M. Then I must have dozed off, because when the door opened and aroused me, the house seemed very still and I had no idea what time it was.

I stared at the doorway. There was a queer ringing sensation in my head, and a tenuous mist seemed to cling to my bulging eyes. Something moved on the threshold. I inched myself higher in bed and leaned forward, striving to see through the mist. Cold sweat began to form on my face.

When I recognized my visitor, my fear abated but my amazement became boundless. I whispered out the name "Hilda!"—and for answer, the woman put a finger to her lips in a gesture that commanded silence. Slowly, then, she closed the door and tiptoed toward me.

The upper half of her pajamas was loose, gaping. The only garment that clung closely to her exquisitely beautiful body was a pair of gossamer-sheer pajama trousers that rustled alluringly as she glided forward. Her pale, full breasts undulated gently under their covering; soft shadows gathered in the velvet vale between them as she leaned toward me.

"You knew I would come," she whispered. "Surely you knew that!"

I remembered then how she had watched me so intently, earlier in the evening. A dozen times our glances had met; a dozen times her dark eyes had seemed to hold a message and a promise. Now I found her lips pressed softly against mine, and my hands caressed the warm, quivering luxury of her half-draped shoulders. I drew her closer to me, and I found myself shaking, quivering with excitement.

In a few moments I had completely forgotten my fears. The room around me was not a chamber in a horror-house but a shadowed rendezvous in some silent paradise where love ruled supreme.

Hilda Lannister's young body was close and warm against mine. Her lips moved against my own and sent waves of desire dancing through my blood. The two arms that I owned were not enough to caress the whole of the velvety body that was straining so impetuously against me.

Lamplight played over the girl's pulsating figure as my hands gently drew her closer. Yellow shadows touched the curving hollows of her waist. We were alone, she and I. Nothing else mattered. I reached out and turned the lamp-wick low....

Later, when I awoke, Hilda was gone, and I became aware of a lingering, heady fragrance in the room. It troubled me. I turned the lamp higher and stared around me. Convulsively I stiffened.

On the crumpled pillow where, not long ago, Hilda Lannister had lain her head, a white flower gleamed evilly in the lamplight!

How long I had been inhaling its deadly perfume, I had no way of knowing. My head seemed strangely large, heavy, and my

*They saw the circle
of blood and stiffened
as if impaled.*

mouth was full of a thick, glutinous substance that threatened to strangle me. That flower! Already I was too well acquainted with its hellish powers! And she had left it here, to destroy me!

I leaped to my feet and went snarling to the door. Something had happened to me since those moments of ecstasy when I had held Hilda Lannister in my arms. I couldn't think straight. My mind now seemed to be gripped by some alien force.

I didn't love Hilda Lannister. I hated her. She had tried to murder me! Now my hands were convulsively opening and closing in their frantic desire to seize Hilda Lannister's throat! At that moment I would have committed murder!

I strode across the dark living-room, through the adjoining room to the staircase. There were bedrooms upstairs. Hilda would be in one of them. She must be destroyed. She was a creature of evil.

Stealthily I crept up the stairs, turned left along the upper landing. Then I stopped.

There was no light here, yet I saw the woman before me as distinctly as if the corridor had been brilliantly illuminated. That fact made no impression on me then. I remember it distinctly now, and know the reason for it. The woman's own body, undraped except for a thin, web-like girdle, exuded a bluish luminescence of its own. A pale, shimmering glow clung to her breasts, to the rapturous curves of her naked thighs. I held my breath, amazed by her beauty. Blood began to pound at my temples.

Arms outstretched, she came slowly toward me. She was smiling. I knew who she was, knew that she was young Trent's widow, Maryata—but I knew, too, that she was no longer merely a woman. She had changed.

An intuition of danger seized me and I took a faltering step backward. Maryata did not stop. Terror seized me. I turned to run. The corridor behind me was blocked with pale, creeping forms which, in sudden madness born of fear, I thought were men.

I stood where I was and screamed. Jones's name and Curtin's name shrieked from my lips as I shouted frantically for help. The only answer was low, mocking laughter from Maryata as the sinister shadow-shapes converged upon me.

Then I saw that my assailants were women, not men! Women like Maryata! The eerie light in the corridor now showed me the unearthly beauty of their gleaming bodies. I stared in amazement.

But theirs was a sinister beauty. Years ago, in the ruins of that jungle city, I had encountered the same kind of evil loveliness and fled from it, terrified. I tried to escape now.

They seized me. When I fought, beating my fists against the flesh of lithe, flawless bodies, they subdued me. Maryata herself bent over me as I lay gasping. Her parted lips found mine and clung there. A feeling of deep lassitude stole over me. In a stupor I caressed the warm, pliant figure that hung close to my tired body, and then, as if drugged by the pressure of her lips, I lost consciousness... not totally, but enough to numb me against any attempts to resist.

They carried me downstairs, through black, gloomy chambers to a large room at the rear of the house. Here again there were no lights, yet the room was eerily illuminated by the weird glow which seemed to emanate from the semi-naked bodies of my female captors. I saw the half-stripped body of John Lannister dangling horribly from an upended table, arms and legs bound, head lolling. I saw a dagger protruding from his sunken chest, and blood dripping to the uncarpeted floor.

I saw Jones and Curtin, both dead, sitting horribly in straight-backed chairs near the wall. Then I saw Hilda.

She screamed as they dragged her forward. When she saw me, and saw that I too was captive, her eyes widened and became dark, dull orbs in a face empty of color. Cruel hands tore the silken pajamas from her lovely body, baring her heaving breasts, her young, resilient flesh. Maryata stepped toward her and stared at her appraisingly, and, with curled fingers, hurt her as only one woman could hurt another.

"Bind her!" Maryata said softly. "It will be a joy to thrust a keen blade into this lovely body!"

Horrified, but helpless to intervene, I watched while they forced Hilda Lannister into a chair. I didn't hate the girl now. Dully I realized that if she had really tried to destroy me, she had surely done so under the influence of a will stronger than her own. My mental anguish was unendurable when I remembered the moments of ecstasy we had spent together in my room.

My own arms had held that young exquisite figure gleaming

now like a statue carved from polished gypsum. My own body had responded to the warm pressure of the form which was now being cruelly lashed to a chair. Dear God, why couldn't I *do* something?

But I hadn't the courage to hurl myself forward. My gaze kept wandering to the dead, ghastly forms of Jones and Curtin, who sat horribly erect on the other side of the room. I kept staring at Lannister, and at the knife protruding from his bloody chest.

Then Maryata began talking.

"**They** are dead now," she said, intoning the words in a kind of chant. "All are dead except this woman they call Hilda and this man who names himself Dykes. Three years we have waited, since that day when I allowed Paul Trent to discover me in Tegulci's village, so that I might accompany him and his companions to their own land and there destroy them. Now...."

She told how, after learning that I intended to buy this old house and call a meeting here, she came here first as a nurse, lived in the house and made all preparations. She told how McClegg, passionately wanting her for his own, had trailed her here, and how she had murdered him and concealed his body in the crypt. "Now," she said, "Hilda Lannister and this man Dykes must die!"

I jerked forward, straining the hands that held me. "Hilda wasn't a member of that expedition!" I cried hoarsely. "You can't include her in your plans for vengeance!"

"She has been told the location of the sacred city," Maryata answered coldly. "Therefore she must die."

Frantically I stared around me. Lannister was dead; he could not help us. Jones and Curtin could not help, either. I had to face this thing alone. But what chance had I against a score of savage women who were planning even now to destroy me?

Maryata was speaking again, and I listened, scowling. The words were in an alien tongue. Recognizing some of them, I stiffened with amazement, held my breath and stared straight at the woman's moving lips. She was addressing her strange followers now, not Hilda and me. And she was speaking in the tongue of a dead civilization, the tongue of the ancient Mayas!

I caught the drift of what she was saying. "By the blood of this man (she meant Lannister) I have summoned you here from the city where death rules. By the blood of the woman (she pointed to Hilda) I send you back. Our work finished. Soon I will join you." I won't swear to the translation, but that was her meaning.

Then she peered at me and spoke in English. "As for you," she said softly, "I find you attractive. There is a way of taking you back with me to the city of ever-lasting death. When we are alone, I will show you."

She drew a long, keen knife from the web-like girdle which was her only garment. Hilda Lannister screamed. Smiling, Maryata advanced slowly toward her, holding the knife in an outstretched hand.

I muttered to myself, in a daze: "These creatures are dead. They are members of an ancient civilization. Dear God, show me a way out of this…." Then I stared at the corpse of John Lannister. In three strides, if I could break loose from the hands that held me, I could reach the table where Lannister's body hung grotesquely in its bonds. I stared at his bloody chest.

Maryata, still smiling, stopped her slow advance and looked down at Hilda's loveliness. "You are very beautiful, my dear," Maryata whispered. "I shall enjoy killing you."

I couldn't move for a moment. I was fascinated by the snakelike movements of the Maya woman's left hand. The hand undulated forward as if to caress the flesh that it threatened. I saw a scream gathering in Hilda's throat, knew that she was struggling to remain brave in the face of death. Maryata's fingers explored the girl's ivory-white shoulders, slid to her throat. The point of the knife hovered over Hilda's heart.

Then, snarling, I tore myself loose and hurtled forward!

The scheme festering in my brain was a fantastic one, based on my knowledge of ancient civilizations. I didn't expect it to work, but my God, I had to do something! A man can't stand still, staring, while a woman is savagely murdered less than ten feet from him!

I hurled myself at Lannister's dead body, raked my right hand across the smear of red blood that covered his chest. Then, whirling to face Maryata as the others closed in on me, I stood there, facing annihilation, and frantically drew a gleaming crimson circle on my own heaving chest. A circle of blood! Hieratic symbol of power and immunity in a civilization long extinct!

Maryata stiffened as if impaled. The knife fell from her hand and she took a faltering step backward, staring at me in horror. Words came from her trembling lips—low, whispered words riding on wings of terror. And then suddenly the strain of the situation was too much for me, after what I'd gone through. I began laughing. I knew that I was alone in the room, that the danger was over, and still I continued to laugh as I stumbled to Hilda's chair and slashed her bonds.

The laughter felt good in my mouth. It was a relief. I tore the last rope loose and lifted Hilda from the chair, led her into the living-room where the big parlor furnace was still burning. I remember hearing her say to me: "You're tired—so very tired. You need rest."

Then I stretched out on the divan and slept, with Hilda's arms around me and my head cradled against the warmth of her shoulder.

It was daylight when I awoke. The doorbell was ringing, and Hilda was not in the room. I pulled a dressing-gown around me and walked stiffly to the door. A man I had never seen before was standing there on the stoop, and he said hesitantly, staring at me: "You're Mr. William Dykes?"

I told him I was.

"Afraid I've got bad news for you," he said. "I'm the brother of Ralph Kern, the fellow you hired to drive your car down to the depot to meet the midnight train last night."

"Yes," I said.

"We found the car in the river," he said dully, "about a hundred yards below the bridge. I guess the bridge was slippery and Ralph was drivin' faster'n he'd ought to, in a storm like that. They're all—dead."

I stared at him. "Dead?" I mumbled. *"Dead?"* and I stood in the doorway, staring after him, as he went down the road.

There was a queer, heavy sensation in my head. It bothered me. I kept mumbling the word "Dead?" as I went wandering through the house in search of Hilda.

The big rear room, where Jones and Curtin had been sitting horribly in their chairs, and where John Lannister's bloody body had hung against an upended table, was empty. Plummer's corpse wasn't in the room where I had placed it. The house seemed to be exactly as it had been before the arrival of my guests last night.

I called Hilda's name and got no answer. "I must be mad," I mumbled. "Mad...."

Then I remembered the crypt in the living-room. With screwdriver and chisel I pried up the boards, lifted them one by one and piled them against the wall. The crypt was there, with its crude wooden ladder slanting down into sinister darkness.

A huge, thick-stemmed vine, festooned with odorous white flowers, grew in the black soil.

MORT LANSING

GREEN EYES

Kyra's eyes lured him, even while her loveliness
repelled him. Yet finally he succumbed.... She had
wanted him to show his love, but when he did....

Thorpe had had too many cocktails. He tried to fight
back the clouds of haze that cobwebbed his brain, tried to
clear the mist from his eyes. Across the table in the crowded
cocktail bar the outline of his companions was growing blurred
and fuzzy. Janice, the woman he had just met, seemed as groggy
as he did. Dizzy as he was, he knew her head was sinking lower
and lower, only to be brought up with great effort while a vague
smile appeared on her lips.

Somehow the second woman, Kyra, gave Thorpe the impression
of being all eyes. Through the swirling smoke and the heady liquor
fumes he could scarcely discern her olive-tinted, heart-shaped
face, the thin crimson blotch that was her mouth. But the long,
green slits, slanted and narrowed, that served Kyra as eyes were
all too vivid in Thorpe's brain. They seemed to peer knowingly,
centuries old in wisdom, to peer unblinkingly, watching and
waiting.

Thorpe needed the job. He hadn't worked for eight months, and
money was low. He fought down the vague feeling of dread, the
unaccountable premonition that something gruesome was about
to happen, and tried to force himself to sobriety. It was no go.
His head sank lower and lower. The muffled conversation of the
room beat at his ears like the roar of surf.

105

A human head stared from the tray, and the girl on the floor screamed piteously.

Stupidly he looked across at the woman, Janice. Quite frankly she was sleeping, her head on her own breast. He mumbled something and made out those slotted green eyes of Kyra peering at him like those of a waiting beast. He half stumbled to his feet, sat down weakly and laid his chin in the palm of his hand, while those green eyes continued to peer at him bleakly, patiently.

Out of the haze came another brown face, a man in a chauffeur's uniform who appeared miraculously; then a brown hand that slid beneath Thorpe's arm to steady him. Kyra was helping Janice in a similar way. Someone at an adjoining table tittered. Thorpe tried to look indignant. The women went first.

With a great effort Thorpe fixed his wavering gaze on the rounded, undulating hips of Kyra. One-two-three-four steps to the whirling door. Be dignified ! Don't be drunken! Too much

depends on this job! Kyra's hips were liquid, flowing and provocative beneath the shimmering thinness of her tea gown.

Now the street. The thing grew hazier than ever. A black limousine waited, next the curb. The strong, helping hand beneath
his arm. Two women, Kyra and Janice the blonde, waiting in the
rear seat, the blonde head bowed in sleep. The softness of the
upholstering, the overpowering sleepiness induced by the cocktails. Thorpe's last thought was that this was a hell of a way to go
out on a new job, a job that meant so much!

He awakened gradually, a little at a time, his brain still fogged
and numbed. The car sped through the darkness. It had been early
evening when they left the hotel. The dashlight showed Kyra in
the front seat beside the brown-faced chauffeur who was talking

excitedly in a foreign tongue. Wakefulness was a great effort. Thorpe closed his eyes, was aware of warmth and softness against his knee.

He opened his heavy lids painfully, made out the dim figure of Janice Marshall in the grey light. She half sprawled, half sat in her corner of the tonneau, her blonde head well back against the cushions. Her body had gradually slipped down, her dress sliding upward, until slender chiffon legs were revealed, topped by gleaming inches of white skin.

Thorpe felt a little sorry for her, started to reach toward the skirt to tug it back in place, when the car stopped. With a sigh he relaxed, was conscious of Kyra's green eyes and the black eyes of the chauffeur peering back at him.

The chauffeur's whipcorded arm slid about Kyra's shoulders. Two figures seemed to merge, the brown face and the olive, the slim shoulders and the brawny. Hazily, Thorpe watched. Clouds still obscured his brain. Kyra's arms were about the man's head pulling him closer and closer to her.

Suddenly metal gleamed in the faint yellow fight. Thorpe's eyes opened a little wider. Again the gleam of metal and the chauffeur's hands tore at the olive face before him. Three times Kyra stabbed downward viciously, cruelly, and the back of the whipcord uniform grew redder at each thrust.

The chauffeur screamed, his face contorted, clawed at the woman, and fell forward against the wheel. Like a flash Kyra was out of the car, around on the other side jerking the door open. She seized the slaughtered man by the coat, dragged him out of the car. Thorpe lost sight of them in the blackness.

He shook his head from side to side, tried to clear it. He was afraid, terribly afraid of this green-eyed death that rode in the front seat of the big limousine. Yet he couldn't move. Through his little remaining consciousness flashed over and over the words, "Dope! Dope!"

For Stewart Thorpe had never been drunk in his life.

By the time Kyra returned to the car Thorpe was sleeping again beside the unconscious girl. Kyra slid into the front seat, threw the car in gear and drove off, her red lips as straight as ever, her green-slotted eyes narrow and cold.

This time Thorpe awakened to the drone of voices about him, knew he was lying on a couch or a bed. The room was in utter darkness except for an electric torch that centered on Thorpe himself. His eyes flickered into the light for a moment. He was conscious of vague shapes that stood about him, cold hands that probed his naked muscles and twisted his big body this way or that. Kyra's voice droned in the blackness.

"He was the best that came in answer to the ad. His measurements are the same, even his weight is almost identical with the other. The facial features, of course, don't matter."

A chuckle in the darkness, a sneering, grating laugh that ran its course along Thorpe's spine. "No, my dear, the face will hardly matter. But his connections, his people? He will be missed?"

"Neither he nor the girl have people or relations in the city. He is from San Francisco; she is from Montreal. There is no danger."

Again those cold fingers, dank like death, probing the chest muscles. Thorpe tried to twist away, to move aside. The light suddenly flicked out plunging the room into darkness. The patter and scurry of retreating feet. A door slammed softly. A key clicked in the lock. Through the window a blood red moon peered knowingly as Thorpe struggled to his feet and shook his befuddled head.

The door was locked from the outside and Thorpe's half-hearted banging failed to budge it. He fumbled along the wall, found the light switch and illuminated the room. It was an ordinary bedroom, magnificently furnished, and for the first time Thorpe took note of his own appearance. He wore a red loin-cloth—nothing more.

For a long time he stared at his reflection in the mirror, noting the vivid contrast of the red cloth against his white skin, then anger surged within him. What the hell kind of joint was this? Get a man out, then take his clothes? He rummaged through the room frantically.

In the closet, a maroon robe, rich and luxurious.

A knock at the door. Hastily he struggled into the robe. The key clicked, a dark-skinned man, scantily clad, his head wrapped in a white turban stood in the doorway. He bowed low, flashed white teeth and turned again to the hall. He reentered pushing a serving table loaded with dishes.

"Listen," began Thorpe thickly, "I've lost my clothes. Who took—?"

The brown man smiled again. "Your clothes," his voice was low, "are being cleaned. You are to refresh yourself before Rogell interviews you."

He spread the little table, so well filled with appetizing food. Thorpe floundered mentally. Had he really gotten drunk or had he been doped? Why dope him? He had answered an advertisement, gone to a hotel, met the woman Kyra, and had been accepted for the job. Why, then, would the woman dope him? Janice Marshall, too had appeared as befuddled as he had. Was she, too—?

"Listen," he said plaintively, "where are we? I didn't feel so good on the way up, went to sleep I guess. Where are we at?"

Black eyes were drilling into his. "You are at the house of Bertrand Rogell, the artist. Presently he will talk to you, will explain everything." Silence while the dishes made a faint clatter on the table. Then again the tense voice of the servant. "While you slept, perhaps you dreamed something? Perhaps you dreamed that Kyra and Manuel, the driver, had words?"

Thorpe raised his brows. A new voice from the doorway. The servant stiffened.

"Why ask that, Achmed? I told you Manuel was left in town to take care of an errand for Rogell. How do you feel, Mr. Thorpe?"

The servant shrugged, pattered out of the room on noiseless feet. Thorpe drew the robe more closely about his shoulders, eyed the woman Kyra with distrust, almost distaste.

He said, "Why do you lie? You didn't leave Manuel in town. I saw it all, saw you kill him as he held you in his arms." He pushed back the table, sprang excitedly to his feet. "I don't know what I've let myself in for but I don't like it. I want my clothes and I want to go back to the city. I think it might be best to take Miss Marshall with me, too, for she isn't safe. If you don't—"

"Drink your wine!" The words were like the crack of a whip. Helplessly Thorpe stood there while those terrible green slots narrowed. Her eyes seemed to swim out of the vague blur of her face, to extend, to stab at him with electric venom.

"I—" he hesitated, dropped his own eyes before the intensity of her gaze. Clumsy fingers fumbled at the thin glass of red wine, raised it to his trembling lips. He gulped it, looked down at the table, his brain whirling.

Her words came flat, low. "You rode out here drunk. You saw nothing—you heard nothing. Look at me and say it."

He looked up, his eyes sweeping from her thin waist, lingering momentarily at her pear-shaped breasts, sliding over the white column of her throat and coming to rest miserably on those green slots. The pupils were distended, enlarged terrifically, seemed to be starting from the iris.

Thickly he said, "I was drunk—I saw nothing—I heard nothing."

She touched his forehead and he started, released from the binding ties of her gaze. She laughed a little and sat down opposite him.

"Eat, Thorpe," she said. "In a few minutes Bertrand Rogell is coming to see you. Obey him in every way and you will not be sorry. Your job—just as I told you in the city—is that of a model. Rogell is painting a series of murals for a certain patron and needs a man and woman like you and Miss Marshall. Tonight he has guests. The two of you are to be introduced, are to mix and mingle with the others. New eat and drink, be refreshed, for there is a busy night ahead."

She was gone. Like a child who has been instructed, Thorpe turned to the serving table, but the food was tasteless. He was too worried to eat. Only the wine, thick and pleasant on his tongue brought refreshment.

Again the door. Again Kyra of the green, hypnotic eyes. Janice Marshall followed her into the room, clutching a voluminous

She laughed at his pain,
not seeing the figure with
the wrench behind her.

Chinese kimono to her slender throat. Her eyes were still blurred but she managed to smile faintly at Thorpe, who nodded a brief hello.

Hardly had the two women been seated when someone knocked again at the door. Kyra called, the knob clicked. Achmed, the brown-skinned servant, entered carrying a man in his arms. Hardly a man, more a monstrosity. He carried the hunchback across the room, set him carefully in a deep chair and moved behind the chair to stand motionless, arms crossed, behind his master.

Bertrand Rogell opened the colorless slot of his mouth and grinned, jagged molars, yellowed and pointed as fangs gleaming against the purple of his tongue. His head was enormous, almost twice normal size, as hairless as an egg, sitting shakily atop his bowed and gnarled shoulders like a misshapen lump of clay. His nose was a shapeless blurb, his eyes tiny and deep set, seeming to hide behind the ghastly folded flesh of his cheek bones.

But when he moved his hands, his features were forgotten. The hands at the ends of the apelike arms were white and soft, with long fingers, beautifully tended and manicured. They were graceful and appealing, like fluttering white birds. He moved them now, as he spoke to the two he had hired.

"Do not be frightened by my appearance, my friends. I assure you though I am foul to look at, my soul is as beautiful as your own!" He nodded his massive head, chuckling.

Thorpe looked over at the girl, Janice Marshall. Her eyes were wide with horror of the monstrosity that was that world-famed artist Bertrand Rogell. The voice went on.

"Your work will not be hard, for I am too weak to paint for long at a time. Your pay, Kyra has explained to you. You will live here at my house, subject to my beck and call, and when my series of murals is completed, you will receive your reward and go. And now my friends I am interested in your bodies. My guests await and we must get to them. You—I believe your name is Janice?—will take the dais."

For the first time Thorpe was aware of the stand in the corner. It was about three feet high, rug covered, the wall behind it hung with a black velvet curtain. At a signal from Rogell the servant turned the lights down, pushed another button that shot a ray of blinding white light across the raised model's stand. The artist spoke again. "You, Miss Janice. I believe you claim to be an experienced model?"

Grimly the girl arose, stepped quickly into the light. Her hair gleamed like spun gold beneath the ray. For a moment she stood there, the kimono drawn tightly about her shoulders and hips, then without a word she dropped it about her feet. Her body was a white lily, slim and straight, emerging from the vivid flame that was the garment.

Thorpe caught his breath, heard the brown servant, Achmed, gasp across the room. The artist purred lake a cat. Kyra's sharp voice broke the tension.

"You will turn, please, slowly."

Slowly the white perfection turned. The arrogant line of the proud breasts—the curving column of the throat—the soft flatness of the muscled abdomen—the sudden flare of the hips—tapering thighs—finery chiseled calves—thin ankles. Proudly she moved, every line of her white body limned against the black wall-covering behind her.

"You, Mr. Thorpe." The words were low. Almost Thorpe refused. But he had modeled much, had no sense of false shame. After all, this man was one of the world's foremost artists, and this woman, Kyra, was his secretary.

Thorpe mounted the dais and dropped his robe. He stood motionless, proud of the perfection of his own body, staring down into the blue eyes of the girl beside him. The scarlet loin-cloth was the only spot of color in the tableau. At a word of command he flexed his muscles until his ribs stood out, until his stomach almost disappeared. Narrow hips, powerful legs, and wide, wide shoulders.

When the light came back on and Rogell waved in dismissal, Kyra's green eyes were intent on the white body of the man.

"The guests await downstairs," said Rogell, and Achmed bore him out of the room.

"We will meet you at the top of the stairs," smiled Kyra, and took Janice Marshall's hand.

"But my clothes," protested Thorpe.

"You will be downstairs but a little while," said the woman. "Rogell is giving a party and everyone is in costume. It is his wish that you appear as you posed."

She was gone leading Janice.

Thorpe cursed. Trust him to get in a mess like this! Damn it all! He poured a drink from the wine decanter. It felt thick and spicy on his tongue. He waited a few minutes, stepped into the hallway.

A white figure huddled at the top of the steps. He hurried toward Janice Marshall, leaned over her. From below came the swirling of soft music, low, provocative, sensual.

"What is it, Janice? What is it?"

"Oh God," she moaned, "I'm afraid, I'm afraid. Why did I come into this?"

He patted her bare shoulder. "Don't be frightened," he said. "You've posed before, haven't you? There's nothing to fear."

"I'm afraid," she whimpered. "Look!"

A curtain of velvet was against the wall, a golden cord hanging from it. She tugged at it with snaking fingers. The curtains spread, revealing a masterpiece, *a masterpiece of pain!* Instinctively, Thorpe's arm slid about the trembling shoulders while his horror-stricken eyes clung to the splotch of color.

In the background, the nude figure of a man lashed upright on a crude cross. Smoke swirled and beat about his abused body in mocking streamers of grey blue that accented rather than obscured the torn flesh of his breast. Long wounds and welts crisscrossed the white flesh from groin to collar bone, from hip to twisted feet.

The head was thrown back in a spasm of agony, the tongue protruded from spittle flecked lips, the eyeballs were rolled so high that only the whites were visible. From the hand on the outstretched right arm blood dripped slowly from five bloody stumps that once had been fingers.

In the foreground, the slender body of a woman with golden hair, bound to a lump of gleaming basalt. The flesh seemed to pulse, the body to quiver with terror. Lips were parted hideously and to Thorpe it seemed almost as if her scream echoed in his ears! Around each splendid breast circled a ring of red, a ring that oozed drops of crimson blood.

Over the body leaned a head and a pair of hands, a head as hairless as an egg, a head whose face was contorted in sadistic glee as long, shapely fingers crushed the soft flesh of a breast flat against the tortured woman, the other hand sliding the point of a cruel knife into the base of the cringing breast. A red worm crawled over the ribs of the victim, dripping onto the basalt to form a gleaming pool.

The torturer was Bertrand Rogell! The picture bore a title—
"PAIN".

Thorpe shuddered, felt gooseflesh crawling all over his body.
With an oath he snatched the golden cord, and the velvet hang-
ings dropped in place. The girl was sobbing at his feet. Fear swelled
in him, fear for himself as well as for this girl. Was this what they
had let themselves in for?

He stooped quickly, picked her up and trotted back down the
hall looking wildly to left and right. She sobbed against his breast.

"Thorpe!" Behind him. Again, "Thorpe!" He set her down, his
teeth chattering. "Rogell wants you to meet his guests."

Smiling, Kyra stood there, her green eyes blazing again.

"That picture," gasped Thorpe. "It's—"

She laid a soft hand on his trembling arm. "You need a drink!
You mean the picture in the hallway? That's a figment of Rogell's
imagination, of course."

He struggled to speak, tried to protest, but her fingers were
tight on his wrist. Janice arose slowly, followed the two of them
to the stairway without a word, her eyes still gleaming with horror.

The room at the foot of the steps was smoke filled, foggy with
incense. Standing in the doorway Thorpe was conscious only of
swirling, uncertain shapes, of low music that throbbed as if from
an infinite distance. Gradually he became more accustomed to
the scene, made out dancers, dancers who were robed in long,
grey garments, whose heads were cowled like penitent inmates
of a monastery and whose eyes glowed strangely behind black
masks.

What kind of party was this? Which were men? Which were
women? Was this fantastic company human? Across the room
he saw the twisted, crouched figure that was Bertrand Rogell, the
artist.

A hand pushed him forward and at the same time snatched
the red robe from his shoulders. He whirled, gazed into the wide,
green eyes of Kyra. Behind her the brown servant, Achmed,
clutched his robe. Kyra pushed him forward gently, and side by

side with Janice he walked toward Rogell.

The music pulsed pizzicato. The dancers paused, made a lane for the two white bodies to pass through. Once a slender hand flicked out to caress Thorpe's biceps. As he turned to glare belligerently, a pair of hot eyes stared at him through the narrow slits of a mask, a red tongue flashed forth to lick at rouged lips.

Rogell sat deep in a throne like chair. A deep red robe hung grotesquely from his twisted shoulders. Long, slender fingers were entwined across his breast. The cruel slot of his mouth twisted in an intended smile of welcome. The music sank lower, his voice rose.

"My friends, I give you—*Beauty!*"

From somewhere high above the yellow finger of a spotlight shot out, bathed the white bodies of the two models as they stood hand in hand before the hunchback artist. Thorpe reddened angrily; Janice gasped, moved closer to him. He stared about indignantly while the spotlight faded to silver, to coral, to orange, to vivid green. He felt the glowing eyes behind the masks, felt the ring of grey figures crowd closer. The light dropped away as suddenly as it came; the music swirled higher.

Hands were on his wrists, hands that jerked him backward. Angrily he tried to turn, glimpsed the face of Achmed over his bare shoulder. Kyra whispered in his ear.

"Do not be frightened. It is a game. Stand against the wall and be quiet."

He stood against the wall quietly but the brown hands never left his wrists.

Janice Marshall stood alone and bewildered before the gargoyle, Rogell. He spoke to her in a low voice, soothingly, too low for Thorpe to make out his words. A curtain at his back parted.

A huge negro towered there, clad in a loin cloth, his torso oiled and gleaming in the sudden light that played on him. He looked like a *geni* out of Arabian Nights. In his hands he bore a huge tray, covered with glistening cloth of gold. With measured tread he moved into the room, bowed once—twice—thrice—and sat the cloth-draped tray on the floor before Rogell. Still bowing he backed away, stood motionless behind the artist, his arms folded.

Rogell spoke to the girl, his tones still too low to be heard across the room. The ring of grey-cowled figures pressed closer. Thorpe stood atiptoe, peering over weaving grey shoulders. Brown fingers bit tighter into his wrists.

Again the music, dropping lower, throbbing in the distance like the faraway beat of tomtoms. Bewildered the nearly nude figure of Janice Marshall approached the tray. She dropped to her knee before it, the long curve from hip to ankle folding into a seductive black shadow. Her fingers touched the gold cloth tentatively, Rogell spoke sharply. She tugged at it timidly, then jerked it aside.

For a moment there was utter silence in the room, then the girl's terrified scream echoed and reechoed from wall to wall, drummed into Thorpe's ears to roar and reverberate again and again. Janice crouched in horror on the floor, one hand covering her mouth, the other clasping a soft breast.

A human head stared back at her from the tray, a head whose white distended eyeballs flickered malevolently, whose twisted mouth gaped open in a spasm of pain, whose neck sat in a chalice that was inch deep in blood, blood that dripped and trickled over the shallow dish onto the tray itself.

Twice the girl screamed and cowered in trembling white beauty on the floor. The echoes died away, almost to utter silence. Thorpe, straining and struggling against the binding brown hands, could hear the shuffle of the grey figures as they strained for a better view, as they whispered and gasped excitedly among themselves. Then again the harsh voice of Rogell.

"That, my friends, will be called *Horror!* Only I, Rogell, can paint a heart that burst with fright on canvas. *Horror!* Indescribable, unspeakable yet paintable! By Rogell!"

Into the circle of light stepped the giant black. Gravely he covered the terrible head, paced sedately back the way he came. Janice cowered sobbing before the artist until the woman, Kyra, touched her shoulder, led her whimpering from the room. And still in the shadows against the wall Thorpe raged and fought the brown hands.

"Let me loose, damn you!" he half sobbed, but the fingers bit deeper. It was Kyra, returning, who touched his shoulder, looked long and steadily into his eyes and took him from the room still muttering.

"The damned beast, to frighten her like that! What does he gain by it? What does he think—?"

"There! There!" she soothed him. "Of course it's just an illusion! The girl wasn't harmed! That's the way Rogell works. He has a photographic eye. The people you see here tonight are his patrons. He shows the scene he means to depict and paints it later—if the bid is high enough!"

"My God!" groaned Thorpe. "What kind of madhouse have I gotten into?"

The alcove was warm, heavy with seductive scent. The light was low, almost negligible. Urged by the gentle fingers of the woman he sat down on the cushioned divan, sank his head in his hands and tried to put the thing together. She

The yellow finger of a spotlight was on them then. A voice said, "My friends, I give you beauty."

thrust a drink into his hand. He gulped it, wondered vaguely at its spiciness. She lay back against the pillows, smiled at him gently, green-slotted, eyes narrow, enigmatic.

"What have you done with Janice?"

"Oh, she'll be all right. It was rather cruel, so unexpected, but tomorrow she'll laugh about it herself when she finds it was a joke, an illusion. She's sleeping in her room right now!"

He sat there in silence, looking at her suspiciously. She had thrown back the long grey robe, far back, exposing the upper slopes of milky breasts. Breasts that rose and fell as she breathed, seductive in their velvet smoothness. One long white leg had emerged from the folds of the robe, pressed closely against his own knee. Instinctively he drew away from her. She smiled.

"Afraid?" It was a taunt, a challenge, a dare.

He tried to keep his head. "After what I saw on the way up here, why shouldn't I be afraid?"

This time she laughed. "You were drunk! You should thank me for bringing you along in that condition. You said you needed the job and I—well—I rather liked the way you looked."

She leaned over and touched his knee. Her fingers were hot.

With trembling hands he pushed her aside, poured himself another drink. He stood up shakily. She arose. The grey robe half dropped into the shadows at her feet. Her body was luminous in the faint light, her green eyes spots of fire. Doggedly he tried to look away, tried to avert his gaze, but her fingers were on his shoulders, arms sliding about his neck.

"Do not be afraid," she half whispered, close to his ear.

The touch of her was like fire. He groaned as she kissed him with parted lips. Slowly his own arms encompassed her, found the fevered softness of her body. Step by step she pulled him backward toward the divan.

Soft music and softer flesh. Sweet incense and sweeter flesh. Maddening wine and more maddening flesh. Thorpe wasn't conscious that the lights were growing stronger, that a circle of peering eyes behind grey masks was closing in about him. He was only conscious of the fact that he was man, that his companion was woman. The harsh voice of Rogell broke into his consciousness.

"*Passion,* my friends, the passion of the primitive. I, Rogell, can give you that, line for line. Burning, pulsing, throbbing, all-devouring, *Passion!*"

Slowly Thorpe staggered to his feet, weak and trembling. The white body of the woman Kyra lay still and silent against the black velvet cushions of the divan. Her eyes burned with an unholy light, her lips were twisted in a smile of contempt. Thorpe turned to the grey-robed circle, wheeled back to the sneering woman.

"Damn you," he grated, "damn you!" With a single stride he was beside her. Fingers sank deeply into her slender throat. The green eyes glowered up at him, the pinpoint lights changing. Her own fingers closed on his wrists, rested there as if in a caress rather than in defense. The red, red lips smiled up at him as something descended on his head with terrific force and all the lights of the spectrum flashed before his eyes.

A tremendous thumping awakened him. Bong! Bong! Bong! At every blow pain wracked his body. It was long moments before he realized that the thumping was inside his head, the throbbing pain of the blow he had received.

Smoke was in his nostrils, in his eyes, in his lungs. He tried to move his arms, found them extended and bound, tried to move his feet and found them lashed painfully together. Gradually, little by little, his pain-addled brain cleared, let him realize that *he hung suspended from a crude cross!*

The smoke swirled aside momentarily. Across the room, straight ahead of him he saw a huge block of glistening basalt, the still white body of a woman bound on it. Again the smoke shifted. He saw breasts that heaved torturously, saw a face contorted hideously with pain and terror, but recognizable as that of Janice Marshall.

He threw back his head and shrieked and the girl's answering scream, as her twisting head allowed her to view his predicament, fought a battle of echoes with his own.

Both were remembering that picture, "*Pain,*" that hung at the top of the stairs.

A door opened and Achmed the brown man entered. Thorpe screamed at him, writhed and twisted at his bonds. The man grinned and went about his work.

On a small table he laid out a gleaming scalpel, a cruelly curved knife and a pointed iron. He brought a charcoal brazier, blew on it with a bellows, and when the coals gleamed red, thrust the pointed iron deep within them. He went out still grinning.

Then Thorpe saw *her*. She slid through the door like a white wraith, her eyes dreamy with the fixed gaze of the opiate eater. Her olive flesh was oiled. It glistened and gleamed in the flickering light as she walked toward him. Her too-red mouth parted in a half smile. She stopped in front of him, her face scant inches away.

He screamed again. Her face never altered.

"You can't do this! You can't do this! It isn't so! It's a dream!" He was remembering the pain-contorted features of the man in the picture, the five bloody stumps on the right hand, the cruel, criss-cross network of welts and scars that disfigured the white body.

"In a little while," she breathed, "they will come down. They, who are rich, will see the picture as it will be! They can buy the picture, but Kyra, Kyra will possess it! Kyra will have it in the flesh!"

She reached out a slender hand, clawed suddenly at Thorpe's mighty chest. He roared as four pointed nails tore four strips of skin from his body. She stood there laughing for a moment, then leaned and kissed the bleeding wounds.

"Kyra, Kyra," she chanted. "Let them have their money to pay for pictures. Kyra takes living flesh! Kyra, Kyra!" Her scented, oiled body revolved miraculously. Her breasts quivered and swayed in the flickering light. Green eyes flashed back again and again to Thorpe who could not tear his gaze away. His tongue protruded, his eyes grew wide with horror as she snatched the scalpel from the table and whirled toward him.

A terrific beating at the door. A hammering, a crashing, the sound of a shouting voice.

She stopped her mad gyrations, leaped for the door, discarding the scalpel for the knife as she passed the table. She jerked open the studded oaken panel. The huge negro tottered into the room, clutching at his breast, his eyes rolling.

"The police! The police!" he gasped and collapsed on the floor. Quickly she barred the door, leaned over him again. His breathing came in great choking gasps as he tried to stem the flow of blood pouring from a bullet wound in his chest.

"That damned Manuel," he managed. "I thought you got him, thought you killed him!"

She crouched back, green eyes flickering for a moment toward the barred door, then back toward Thorpe. "I knifed him and left him in the swamp," she said, but the negro did not hear her. He was dead.

Like a cat she crouched and glided toward Thorpe. Again he bellowed like a frightened bull, but she shook her head.

"This will be all, this will be the end. I felt it today, somehow. Still Kyra will not die without her picture! Your body! It is magnificent!"

The knife flashed. Thorpe groaned as the razor-sharp point swept down his ribs leaving a bleeding train in its wake.

Again a pounding at the door. Again Thorpe screamed, terror lending volume to his shrieks. She laughed.

"The door will hold until I finish, my friend. We will go to hell together, the three of us, and Kyra will take her picture with her!"

The knife slid toward his right hand where it was bound on the crosspiece. The blade bit into his writhing fingers and she laughed at the spasm of pain that crossed his face. Deeper and deeper she pressed and at the same time brought her lips closer and closer to his until they pressed his mouth as hotly as the knife pressed his writhing hand.

Over her head he saw the spectre. Through the swirling smoke it came, mud-covered, blood-covered, brown face thick with ooze and slime. In its hands, a huge wrench, upraised, ready to strike. *Manuel, the chauffeur, whom this woman had left for dead in a swamp.*

Thorpe tried to roll his head away. The woman sensed danger like an animal, turned swiftly, but too late to avoid the descending wrench. She snatched at the knife and it bit through the thong that held Thorpe's wrist. With a sickening crunch the great wrench met her skull.

She tottered, stumbled and collapsed. The spectre leaned over her, wrench raised for another blow. The beating at the door became more violent. They were using something for a battering ram. Thorpe twisted on his cross, worked frantically at the binding on the other hand as Manuel struck again.

"Killed me! Dead am I! You witch!" *Thump! Thump! Thump!* The black hair was slowly turning to a welter of red and ghastly grey. "Manuel is hard to kill! I crawled to the highway and flagged a car!" *Thump! Thump!* "I bring the police! I know where to find you, I know the secret entrance to this place!" *Thump!*

Horrified, nauseated, Thorpe dragged the thong from his ankles just as the door crashed open. A blue-coated policeman pulled the half-dead Manuel from the battered thing that once had been Kyra, of the green eyes.

A detective looked down at the corpse. "Jeeze," he said, awed, "the guy must have hated her plenty!"

From the doorway Achmed, the other brown man, spoke. He was handcuffed to an officer.

"He didn't hate her. He loved her. She was his wife."

The head of Mike Vasco

The girl wasn't so gay when she talked
about the condemned man. It was she who
had applied at the prison for his body....

I was especially interested because I'd just returned from an expedition into the Amazon region of the Jivaro Indians—the true head hunters. I was intrigued, too, because the girl was damned beautiful; and farther, because *I* happened to have been the shamus on the New York force who had cinched the case against "Count" Mike Vasco four years ago and sent him to the chair.

Chick Dunbar, crime reporter on the *World-Telegram,* had told me the little Italian restaurant where I might find her.

"It'll give you some dope for your book on heads, and," Chick grinned, "wait till you see Kittie Wilson."

I didn't have to wait so long. That night before midnight I was paying for her wine over a red-checkered table cloth at Vando-ni's—and right away I knew I was going places with that baby... and doing things, if I hadn't lost *all* my luck!

She had that kind of hair that movie stars wish they were born with; looked like soft waves of captured bronze flame, and it was real. Her eyes were green with tiny gold dots, and they seemed to be full of devils waiting to stir up a little palatable hell. She had been Mike Vasco's girl.

As a matter of fact, I remembered dimly having seen her picture, though she took no part in the trial, and didn't recognize

"I haven't told you the worst," she murmured.

me.

The wine was giving a tempting flush to her cheeks.

"It's funny I haven't met you before," she mused. "I know nearly all the newspaper guys."

"I've been out of the country," I explained hastily. "Just got

back… but there's nothing to keep us from making up for lost time, is there, baby?"

She grinned saucily. "Not a thing, mister!"

She was small, but her figure was a knockout. Cute and cuddlesome, like a kitten; my hands began itching to touch her. Kittie knew what I was looking at when she leaned farther over the table. The thin sweater she was wearing didn't show any signs of a brassiere underneath, and her pert little breasts swayed as she leaned; they looked too good to be real, but they were. She caught my hand, lying on the table, and brushed it to her breast in a swift caress, then dropped it.

"Whew!" I breathed. "Baby, that's the works with me." She laughed softly.

"But," I went on, "Chick said you could give me a good story about Count Mike Vasco."

A swift shadow crossed her face, and a stab of pain seemed to drive the light out of her eyes for a moment. She put her hand to her forehead, looked down at the table. After a few seconds, she said, very low: "All right. I like you. I'll tell you."

I ordered more wine.

"Mike," she told me, "really had more to him than the police gave him credit for. He knew he'd get the hot seat some day—and he prepared for it."

"You mean he took out plenty of insurance, and all that sort of stuff?"

She didn't answer me directly. "I suppose you think it's hooey," she said, lifting her eyes to mine, "about dying and then coming alive. But did you ever hear of suspended animation?"

"You mean this stuff you hear about in India? Fakirs getting buried and then reviving?"

"Something like that. And it can be done. Not only there.... Ever hear of the *zombie* business, in Haiti?"

"I've even seen them," I told her, "and touched them."

"Then you'll believe me," she rushed on eagerly. "A hypnotist puts the native into a trance till he looks dead, and then after burial, he digs the poor creature up and makes him work after reviving him only partially."

"You've got the straight dope," I told her.

"Well, Mike could do things like that. At least he said he could. I never saw him do it on anyone but himself; but he could make his own body cold and stiff as a corpse, so that you couldn't feel any sign of life or a pulse. He could snap out of it in a few minutes and have a drink with you."

The word seemed to remind her, and she took a sip of wine.

"So that was Mike's swell plan. He knew they wouldn't electrocute a dead man, so all he'd have to do would be to die and cheat the chair. He could be dug up later by someone in the know.

"So when he finally was slated for the works, and they had him up in the little house at Sing Sing, he had me come to see him, and he told me that he was going to die, and that the prison physicians would pronounce him dead and would give me the body if I made application. I was to go through with the funeral and dig him up some days later.

"I knew he could do it," said Kittie reflectively. "And he did. He went out cold. Stiff as a corpse. Several doctors pronounced him dead, and of course the execution was off."

Kittie's voice had grown a little grim, and I felt a cold sweat breaking out on my forehead. Here was something about the Mike Vasco case that I didn't know! The man I thought I'd sent to the chair hadn't been executed after all. I'd been out of the States at the time, having resigned right after the conviction, and had just taken it for granted.

"And so?" I asked, my mouth feeling dry.

She glanced down at her wine and then at me. She smiled queerly. "For the rest of the story," she said enigmatically, "you'll have to come up to my room. It's not far from here...."

I swallowed. Getting invited to go up and see Kittie wasn't bad. What had I been looking for, anyway? But on the other hand there was something queer about all this dope about Mike Vasco. I had an idea.

"Okay, honey," I said smoothly. "That listens sweet to me." We got up to leave. "Only," I went on, "you'll have to excuse me just a moment. Telephone call."

That was right. I wanted to make one. I did. I called up Tate Murphy, detective captain. He'd been a lieutenant four years ago.

"Listen, Murph," I said, "this is Reilly. Yeah. Oh, sure, I'll be around to chew the rag tomorrow. What I want to know now is this: did Mike Vasco actually get the juice when we sent him up or not?"

After a moment I hung up slowly.

Vasco, according to Murphy, had kicked off two days before the fatal date. There had been no execution.

I went back to Kittie. She had plenty to do to make me forget that I wanted to hear the rest of that story *pronto*. But she had a game, and she knew how to play it.

She lived in a small flat, one story walkup. She threw herself back on the divan so that her skirt fell back above her knees, disclosing the best looking pair of legs I'd ever seen.

"You're a newspaper guy now, aren't you?" she purred.

"Not exactly," I said cautiously. "I'm working on some features, that's all."

"You think my story will help you any?"

"If it does," I said, coming directly to the point she was driving at, "I'll give you a cut on the heavy sugar."

"In advance?"

"I don't look so easy as all that, do I?" I laughed.

She pouted. "Come here," she commanded softly.

I didn't object to that. I sat down beside her.

"I like you, anyway," she murmured. "This is what I've been wanting you to do all evening."

She took one of my hands—it was already a little shaky—and held it to the warm mound of her right breast. I could feel her take a sharp gasping breath as I squeezed gently. She threw both arms above her head and closed her eyes, and I did something I'd been thinking about. I caught the waistband of the thin, tight sweater, and pulled it up almost to her shoulders.

I was right. There was nothing underneath except Kittie. Her little breasts quivered just below the sweater. I touched the soft cones that seemed almost to throb and pulsate with pounding blood, and drew my finger tips over them in light teasing patterns.

Her skin was warm and satiny to the touch, and she seemed as fragile as a doll when I put my hands under her arms and caressed her; her ribs were thin and flexible, and I could feel them bend like a baby's.

I thought her eyes were still closed, but after a minute I saw her looking at me intently. She smiled. I grinned back at her.

"You know a few little—tricks, don't you?" she breathed.

"You have," I told her, "seen absolutely nothing... yet."

"Show me more," she urged.

I did. I showed myself more. That skirt had an uncanny way of taking itself off her. Underneath she had on a pair of powder-blue step-ins that were as transparent as any alibi I'd have given for taking a look at them.

Kittie had been hiding the niftiest pair of hips in New York. They gave an impression of being soft and warm and round, and at the same time lithe and smooth and made for movement.

She must have known that I was no sap when it came to recognizing class.

"Well?" she drawled.

"Damn well!" I breathed huskily.

She laughed softly and crossed her knees. I reached down and slipped off both her shoes. Then took hold of a stocking top and started peeling it down past her knee....

When I did that, she sat up suddenly and threw both her arms about my neck. She was breathing very fast. So was I. I finished pulling the sweater off over her head and started kissing her throat and then her mouth. Her tongue was like a sip of hot honey.

When too many shivers jittered down my spine, I went back and completely took her stocking off.

"Okay," I told her half an hour later, "if the rest of the story is any good, I'll give you twenty-five smackers for it."

Kittie leaned back in the easy chair and crossed her legs. I could see the smooth curves of her knees and thighs beneath the negligee. I didn't want to begin getting ideas again so soon. I looked away.

"Cash?" she asked coolly.

"Cold fish," I told her. "On the spot."

When she started telling about Mike Vasco again, Kittie was like a different woman. Her face grew white, her lips drooped and trembled slightly, and her eyes lost their merry gleam.

"I told you there was no execution," she said dully.

"Yes.... Did you get the—the body all right?"

Kitty shrugged. "I got a promise of it without any trouble at all. I was passing as his wife. But there was one thing—"

"They discovered the trick," I suggested.

"No." She looked up sharply. "Remember Nino?"

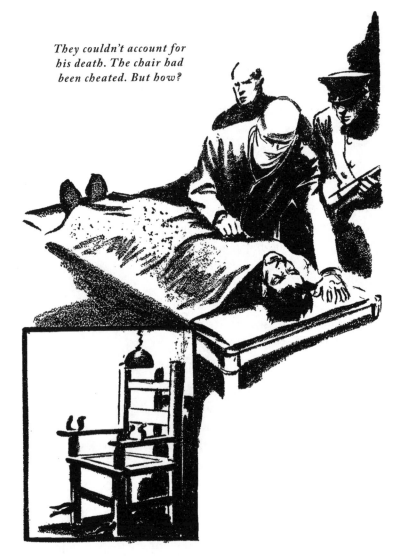

They couldn't account for his death. The chair had been cheated. But how?

"You mean that little spick who followed Mike around?"

"He was South American," she said quietly. "Mike had saved his life once, and he stuck to Mike like a hound dog. He got rubbed out last year," she said reflectively.

"But what about Mike?" I asked impatiently. "You said the doctors pronounced him dead."

She said bitterly: "But none of them could give the cause. I guess that's why they had an autopsy."

"God!" I muttered. My tongue felt dry. I slipped my arm about her shoulders. She looked up.

"But that's not all," she said slowly. "The doctors gave me... his *head!*"

She jumped up suddenly and drew in a sharp breath. "Nino," she told me, "did something to it, the way the head hunters do, to reduce it. I couldn't watch."

"I know. Hot sand and skill and patience," I told her. "It takes days and sometimes weeks."

"Anyway," she shrugged, "that's all I ever got of Mike."

"What!" I felt the skin prickle along my spine.

"His head," she repeated dully.

She went to the divan on which we had been a few minutes before. She lifted up one cushion and slipped something out. She held it out to me, and I took it gingerly. It was a ghastly thing.... The hair was long in comparison to the size of the head, and you could tell it was a white man; though of course there've been white heads cured before. The lips were sewed shut. I handed it back to her. Then I took out twenty-five iron men and gave them to her.

"*Swell* girl, Kittie, huh?" Chick Dunbar gave me a sly grin, next day when I dropped into his apartment. "Did you see"—his grin faded entirely to awe—"Mike Vasco's head?"

I looked blank. "Did you hear that story?"

"Me and two other fellows. We paid her for the exclusive rights to it—but you can use it in your book. No articles."

"You believed it—all of you?" I asked.

"It is weird," he admitted, "but true."

"There are a couple of small catches to it," I said cautiously. "One of them is that in an autopsy they chop the head open, too. Ever think of that? Another is that—well, I don't know how true the rest of the yarn is. They never did find what Mike died of, so Murphy tells me. But this head of Kittie's is a little too pat. She probably hasn't got the nerve to examine it too closely herself or she would have taken out the little sticker inside the neck that says 'Made in Panama—45 pesos.' It's just a tourist's souvenir."

...But of course *that* was just a yarn too—a trick of mine to keep Chick from using the story. There hadn't been any sticker in that head at all—and it *did* look like Count Mike Vasco. I can't explain all the facts. The only thing I know is that I went to see Kittie Wilson *once* more. I left *pronto*... because she was still sleeping with that head under her cushion.

LEW MERRILL

BAT MAN

Was he animal or was he human? Sometimes
he loved the woman who had been his fiancee;
at other times he cared only for his furry mate.
What had happened to John Charters?

The glare of the lights terrified and blinded me. I crouched there, in a corner of the room, looking at the empty bed, and seeing, in the corridor beyond, women in nurses' uniforms passing from room to room.

I tried to fly, and discovered that my left wing was injured. I could only crouch there, shaking with terror, in spite of my frantic desire to fly round and round the walls of the little room, in search of some refuge beyond the reach of earth-bound creatures.

I saw a nurse with golden hair pass along the corridor, and that hair of hers seemed to me a haven of rest. If only I could fly to it and conceal myself within it!

For I had become a bat. A bat with a man's intelligence, a man's memories, striving to emerge from a confused mass of jumbled recollections.

"He's got the brain of a bat." Who had said that? Roger Dean, who had transformed me into this low form of life, by grafting my brain into the body of one of my species. Roger Dean, who was jealous of me, and wanted to supplant me with Alice!

I had been ill a long time, but I couldn't remember just what had been the matter with me. I recalled vaguely that there had been business troubles, a quarrel with Alice. I had even thought

135

of suicide.

What did it matter? I was a bat now, and soon they would discover that I had escaped from them, and they would catch me and put me in a cage, and rob me of my blessed freedom. For we bats are only able to live in freedom. You can't cage us. We die. And Roger Dean wouldn't want me to die. He wanted to gloat over me, and show me to Alice.

If only my left wing hadn't been broken!

Something tapped softly against the window-pane. I looked up and saw another bat, and knew that it was my mate. I scrambled up the window-sill, my tiny, furry body creeping beneath the shade so silently. Then I heard a startled cry from the room. It was the golden-haired nurse.

"He's gone!" she cried. "He's gone!"

But I had already scrambled down the wall and was outside the hospital. Densely dark though the night was, I could see as well as by day. My mate was flitting and circling overhead, and I let her guide me. In a few minutes, scurrying on the ground, making

such short flights as my wing permitted, I had passed beyond the boundaries of our little town, and was making for the old, abandoned quarries on the outskirts.

I knew them well, for, as a boy, I had traced their labyrinthine passages.

My mate circled above me, and then, with a thin shriek, darted inside. As I followed, scrambling with my bad wing, a delicious odor began to come to my nostrils, growing stronger and stronger as I penetrated to the inmost recess of the labyrinth. The odor of warm, soft bodies like my own.

The space above me was filled with the darting creatures, issuing after insects, and returning, but there were scores that remained hanging head downward from the rocky roof of the cave, splotching the walls with their dark, downy bodies. These, I knew, were mother bats, nursing their young.

Right in the midst of them was a vacant space that I knew was mine. No, ours!

I climbed up the rocks, and was welcomed with twitterings of satisfaction at my arrival. I hung there among my fellows. Day was already dawning, and, as the dim light began to filter into the labyrinth, the remainder of the brood returned, clinging to the rocks until they covered them.

Their sleeping-time had come. The gibbering and the twittering ceased. Oh the happiness that I felt, now that I had found my own! The sweet scent, the sense of solidarity among us, as if one single mind animated us all.

Then, with a little whimpering sound, my mate crawled to my side and clung to me, fastened herself to me, her downy body against my own.

I must have slept through the day. I awoke to find that it was dark again. And with that awakening a dim remembrance of the past came back to me. God, I had once been a man—that brain of mine that Roger Dean had transplanted into the skull of a hideous bat! I had loved Alice, and this had been his revenge!

And here I hung in my loathsome bat-form, locked tight in the embrace of my mate, which had never ceased to cling to me through those hours of sleep. I was shut off forever from the world of human beings, from the woman whom I still loved with my human brain, though she seemed very far in the past. I must go to her, and find whether she had married Roger Dean.

Besides, with my awakening hunger, a new instinct was awakening in me. I wanted to see Alice asleep, and apply my mouth to that pretty throat of hers, drawing out the warm blood until my thirst was appeased, yet so gently that she wouldn't know.

They say the vampire bat lives only in South America. But the instinct is latent in all of us. And how could I catch insects on the wing, crippled as I was? The taste of warm blood from Alice's veins would almost recompense me for having become the thing

I was.

Already my companions were beginning to squeak and gibber as their waking time arrived. The thing that had been clinging to me now detached itself, and flitted spectrally out through the opening of the quarry. The rest took wing also. I worked my way down to the ground and began moving silently through the streets of our town, until I reached the one on which Alice lived.

The town was dim to me, though I could see plainly in the darkness. But it required a constant and immense effort of mind to recall the days when I had walked its streets, a human being.

God, how I hated Roger Dean, when I was able to recall what he had done to me!

I would have fastened my small, keen teeth in his throat and drawn the life-blood out of it, except for Alice. She had been so gentle and compassionate. I was sure she would give me of her blood, if she knew who I was.

I reached what I thought was the house, and, scrambling up the clapboards, perched myself upon the sill, and peered in through the open window. The room was quite dark to human eyes, but perfectly visible to mine.

I saw a man and a girl embracing each other, holding each other fast in an ecstasy of passion. I could hear them speaking in low tones, and, bat though I had become, I understood what they were saying to each other.

"**Roger,** darling, I'm so happy with you," the girl was saying. "Just think, it's a whole month since we came back from our honeymoon, and we care for each other more than ever, don't we!"

I heard his voice answering, and recognized it. It was that of Roger Dean, my murderer and my rival. So he had won Alice? For a few moments the blind, impotent rage of a bat filled my heart as I realized how helpless I was.

But then the girl turned her face, laughing up into her husband's eyes, and I realized that she wasn't Alice, but a strange girl. I could see her long, smooth limbs, her breasts, crushed in the man's embrace, and her dark hair. A stranger!

So Roger Dean had discarded Alice, after performing that vile operation on me!

"You know, darling, I used to be terribly jealous of that Alice Drew," said the girl. "I was afraid you cared for her, after I had begun to love you. You did at one time, didn't you?"

"That was before I met you, sweetheart."

"And you're quite sure that you don't care for her a little bit still?"

"She's a good friend, and I want you two to be friends. But she was never anything to me from the moment that I set eyes upon you."

"That was a week after poor John Charters escaped from the hospital, wasn't it? Poor Alice, it must all have been a dreadful shock to her. Would he ever have got well?"

"Well, he had about the brain of a bat," answered Roger Dean. "A human brain functioning—what there was of it—by blind instinct. It would have been interesting to see what would have happened if he hadn't escaped and fallen into the river."

"Do you think that was his body they found?"

"Well, the head was battered out of all semblance to any human head, when the cataract carried the body over the rocks. Yet it must have been poor Charters, or he couldn't have escaped re-capture—poor Charters, with his bat-brain. Don't let's talk about him, dearest. Kiss me again."

Her arms went around his neck, and she strained herself to him. I watched them, mad with fury.

She knew what he meant when he spoke of my "bat-brain." She, too, was laughing at me.

I must have made some sound, for suddenly she had started out of his arms. "Roger, what was that?" she screamed. "At the window! Look, look!"

Silently as a bat moves, I dropped from the sill and fluttered to the ground. I heard Dean shouting, and presently he came running out of the front door with a gun in his hand.

But at that same time I was hanging, quite invisible to him, in the shrubbery, beside the house. After a while he went in again and closed the door.

"There's no one around here," I heard him call. "It must have been the wind at the shutter, dear."

"But I was sure I saw— I was sure I saw—" I heard her say.

My brain was working furiously; my bat's brain, through which the human emotions were trying to force a channel of thought. Why couldn't what Dean had left of it—why couldn't it function as a human brain? Were the obscure vital processes of the bat gradually destroying the human element in it? I remembered how those two had clung together, and I remembered Alice, and the quiver of a man's desire ran through my furry body. For a while I hung in the shrubbery, shaken by passion. Then I dropped to the ground and edged softly out into the night again.

In a few minutes I had reached what I was sure was Alice's house. Again I climbed to the window and looked inside.

In the darkness I could see a girl's form lying in a bed, a thin sheet halfway over her. She was asleep, and breathing smoothly and regularly.

Very quietly I moved across the floor, trailing my broken wing, then climbed one of the bedposts and perched myself upon the pillow. The girl's face was turned away from me, but I was sure that she was Alice.

The night was warm, and only a single sheet partially covered her. I could see her body in the rumpled, sheer nightdress, the rounded orbs of her breasts, one of which drooped softly against her arm, while the other pointed invitingly toward me. A sweet, warm fragrance came from her naked throat and shoulder, making me forget the sweeter fragrance of my companions in the cave. For a moment I felt a man again.

Through the nightdress was faintly limned the flattened oval of her stomach, the curve of her full hips; underneath the edge of it the whiteness of her thighs. They were crossed, and she seemed to be dreaming happily, for there was a look of rapture on her face.

I had crept down from the pillow, to draw some blood from her, without awaking her, as we bats know how to do. All the infernal instincts of my race were alive in me. And yet—even then

I had that strange illusion that I was once more a man.

I even fancied that, instead of perching there near her white throat, a little, furry creature, I was a man beside her, clasping her around her slender waist, and pressing my lips to hers.

But this wasn't Alice!

I could see her face as she stirred. It was that of a woman in her early thirties, a sensuous face. And her body quivered sensuously as I applied my lips to her warm skin.

"Is that you, darling?" she whispered. "How daring of you, coming in here tonight!"

She smiled, and slowly raised her arms and closed them about the place where my neck would have been, if I had been a man. She strained her body against where mine would have been, and I could have sworn for the moment that I was a man, and that our lips met in a throbbing kiss.

Suddenly she shrank back, and her eyes dilated. "Who are you?" she whispered in terror. "You're the—the man who breaks into houses at night and makes love to strange women, aren't you?"

But I couldn't answer her, of course. She was still half asleep. And I was absorbed, searching for a place to apply my keen little teeth. I saw the tracery of blue veins on her neck, and I was mad with the desire for blood.

"It doesn't matter," she whispered. "I adore you for your daring."

Suddenly she shrieked as I nipped her, twittering with ecstasy, shrieked and leaped from the bed.

I heard her stumbling down the stairs, calling for help, and then the sound of running footsteps. But, again, for me escape was easy. I scrambled to the open window, was down the clapboards of the house in a moment, and running for the shelter of the trees in the little park.

I couldn't understand how I had got confused. By this time I was too frightened to try to find Alice again that night. I made my way back to the quarry, and sought my old resting-place. The bats were flitting in and out by scores, and, as I found my niche, a soft, furry body flopped beside me, and an insect was thrust into my mouth.

I swallowed it mechanically, and mechanically my mouth opened again to receive another of the loathsome delicacies. My mate was bringing me food, because my wing was crippled, and I was unable to hunt for myself.

Through the remainder of the night I clung there, my mouth opening mechanically like a fledgling's, whenever she appeared beside me to thrust in another insect. To me the taste of that food was delicately rare, horrible as the memory of it is now, for by this time Alice and the past had grown very faint again. I exulted in the companionship of my fellow bats, as they winged their way in and out of the cave, bringing food for their young. I felt my consciousness go out to the tribe, unite, and become one with them.

When at last dawn was approaching, my mate ceased to feed me, and snuggled up to me again. There we hung, heads downward, our bodies close together.

With dawn, the bats came winging back to sleep. Soon the wall of the rocks was once more covered with a dense cluster. Now I had forgotten everything. I lapsed into unconsciousness.

Days, weeks seemed to go by. I had forgotten Alice, for my mate was feeding me. And then, suddenly the desire for blood awoke in me once more.

Then one night I found myself in the street, crouching beneath Alice's window. I realized my former mistake. I had confused left and right. I had gone to the wrong side of the little park. Now I had found her.

There was no light in her window, but it was open, and, when I had clambered to the sill, to avoid startling her, I tapped, tapped with my sound wing until I heard her movements within the room. Then she said, in a steady tone:

"Who's there? Don't move! I've got a revolver. I think you're caught at last!"

"It's I. It's John Charters!" I tried to say, though of course only a thin twitter came from my mouth.

"Merciful God!" I heard her whisper.

A little shaded light beside her bed went on, and I saw her sitting on the bed looking at me, her fair hair falling about her neck, and her lovely breasts half-bare.

"John! John!" she whispered, looking at me in mingled horror and pity.

She knew me! The very force of my love had somehow enabled us to communicate by telepathy with each other. Furry, repulsive little thing though I had become, as I scrambled toward her bed, she knew that the soul of me was the soul of the man she had loved.

Silent, rigid, white, she waited till I had scrambled up the bedclothes and perched myself upon the bed beside her knee.

"Alice," I twittered, "I see you know me. I want you to believe what I'm going to tell you. Can you understand what I am saying to you?"

And again she understood me, though my words were only the shriek of the flittermouse I was!

"Yes, John, I understand you," she answered.

"Roger Dean made me what I am, because he was jealous of our love. He operated on me in the hospital, removed my brain and placed it in the skull of a bat. I am a man in a bat's body, Alice!"

What a glance, what a piteous glance she gave me, as if she had suspected all! I saw her open her lips as if to speak, then check herself.

"I'm glad that devil didn't marry you. I saw him with that woman he married."

"You? That was you?" she whispered in real terror.

"Yes, I have been looking for you so long. Oh, my dear, I was so afraid something had happened to you. If I were a man, I should ask you to let me creep into your arms and lie there. Would you?"

"Why, of course, John, darling," she answered.

"But I'm a bat, you see. I live in the quarries, and I have a mate who brings me food. Am I frightening you?"

She fixed me with that steady gaze of hers. "No, John, go on," she whispered.

"You're not afraid that I'll get into your hair?"

"No, I'm not afraid. But you can have my hair, darling. Anything you want of me."

"Oh, if only I was a man again," he sobbed. "Alice, don't be frightened when I tell you what I want. I want to drink some of your blood. May I?"

"Why, of course, John," she answered softly. "Come here to me!"

I scrambled toward her, little broken thing that I was, and nestled close to her lovely shoulder—so white, so soft and warm. Oh God, if I had been a man instead of a loathsome bat!

I put my tiny, fox-like head against her smooth throat and

nuzzled there, and felt her cool hands pressing against my face, stifling the throbbing in my brain. I put my lips to her white flesh and drew a tiny fold between my sharp little teeth. The skin broke as I nipped it.

And then somehow I knew—it was just as if it had been shouted in my ear—that all my immortal future depended upon the fight which had suddenly been forced upon me. If I drank of Alice's blood, there would be no hope for me throughout all eternity. If I abstained, I might hope some day, somehow, to win back to human form, if not in this incarnation, then in a subsequent one.

I drew my lips away. "I've hurt you, dear," I twittered.

"No," she answered. "You couldn't hurt me, John. Do anything you please to me. But let me hold you close."

I snuggled down again, and she crooned over me like a mother. Gradually my thirst for her blood abated. I was winning that fight.

I caressed her skin with my claws, fondled her smooth throat, and stroked her hair, thinking all the while how great her love must be, that she could endure such a repulsive little thing so close to her. Then I lay passive, and let her fondle me.

"Your arm, darling, isn't it better?" she asked.

You see, she had even called my wing an arm. She was pretending that I was a man!

"Not yet," I answered. "That's why my mate feeds me. I must go back to her, Alice, and you must forget me."

"Back to the quarries, John?"

"Back to the quarries, never to see you again. I realize how I have hurt you, coming here like this. It would have been better to have let you go on thinking me dead."

"I knew you hadn't died, darling. If you had died, I should have known. I'm coming with you, John."

Remember, all this conversation was carried on by pure telepathy. How could she have understood the meaningless squeaks that issued from my lips, save through the telepathic powers of love?

"I can't—I can't let you come there," I said.

"But you can't drive me away. I'm coming, John," she answered.

"To—to see me living there? I told you I—I've got a mate there. It's not for human beings. And when I'm there, I—I forget. I become wholly a bat again. You couldn't understand the—the beauty and the glory of it."

"I'm coming with you, John," she answered. "Don't be afraid of me. My sister's away, and there's no one else in the house. Wait till I'm dressed, and I'll come with you."

"I'll wait outside," I said, and perched myself upon the windowsill.

I had always known that Alice was no prude, just the sincerest, simplest, sweetest girl in the world. Why should she have wanted to hide her lovely body from a bat, even though it had a human brain? She seemed forgetful of herself entirely.

She turned away as she stripped the nightdress over her head, but that was all. I devoured her soft, boyish bosom with my eyes, and the lovely curves of her hips as she put on step-ins and stockings. And, like so many women, she sat on the floor to put her stockings on. I don't know why this little thing touched me so deeply.

Then she slipped the dress over her shoulders and put on her shoes.

"I'm ready, dear John," she said. "Let's go downstairs."

"It's easier for me to climb down the front of the house," I answered. "I'll wait for you outside."

"Oh!" she gasped, pressing her hand to her breast, and I saw the tears come into her eyes.

But I was already scrambling out of the window, and I was hardly down before the front door opened, and Alice came out. I scurried along beside her, looking up into her eyes with eager hope. Could she really be coming to the quarries, to live there with me? Could a human being understand the joy and the wonder of the bat life?

"If my wing, would heal, I could fly," I said.

"Oh, John, don't speak about it," she sobbed.

*"There he is,"
she cried. "Don't
hurt him!"*

So I said nothing more, but fluttered along beside her, looking
up into her face every now and then to reassure myself that she
wasn't weakening.

I was sure she would be afraid when we reached the entrance
to the quarries, with the bats skimming in and out, but she only
put both hands on her hair and followed me.

Then at last, in the dim recesses, I stopped. We could only just see the dim outlines of each other. I'm not sure that she could see my wretched little furry form at all.

"My place is on that wall," I said. "You cannot see it now, but it is just visible in the daylight."

She broke down then, convulsed with sobbing; sat down on a rocky ledge and sobbed and sobbed as if her heart was broken. I tried to comfort her, but nothing that I could say made any difference.

"That scoundrel, Dean, should pay for his wretched work," I said, "but I'm only a bat. What can I do?"

"John, have you been living here these past three weeks?" she asked.

"Three weeks? About three days," I answered. "Ever since I escaped from the hospital."

"John, will you come with me—to a place where—you will be comfortable? No more hunting for food in garbage cans at night, and—"

"You mean the zoo," I said. "No, no, my dear, I prefer my liberty. And you're quite mistaken about the garbage cans. My mate brings me my food, because I cannot fly. I sleep all day, and it is warm and comfortable among the bats. Oh, the great peace and joy of it—if you could only know, Alice!"

She was silent for a while. Then she said, in a strained tone:

"Shall I find you here, John, when I come back?"

"You're going away?" I hadn't thought she would stay, but that hurt me.

"I've got to go away. I wasn't prepared. But I'll be back soon. You'll stay here, won't you, John?"

"Yes, I'll stay here," I answered.

I was hanging head downward among the rocks again, and my mate was twittering beside me. She seemed to sense that something unusual had happened, something that threatened my safety. And, because there is only a single consciousness among the bat tribe, the others seemed uneasy too.

I still remembered Alice, but in a dim way, for the blessed dawn was coming, when I could sleep and forget. I should be snugly asleep in this dark, secret paradise. I was already snuggling into my mate's embraces when there arose a sudden commotion in the cave.

Though it was dimly light, the bats were rising in scores from their resting-places, and flitting to and fro, squeaking and gibbering, till the whole interior of the quarry was alive with wings.

Then I discovered what the cause was. Three men were entering the cavern, with flashlights in their hands. The dreadful light blinded me, and terror overcame me, but, with my broken wing, I could only cling to the wall.

And now the bats were streaming out over their heads, leaving me alone. Even my faithful mate had deserted me.

"There he is!" I heard one of them say, and the torchlight, directed full at my face, was agony.

"Oh, take care! I'm afraid he'll fall! Don't let him fall!" cried another voice, in a high-pitched key.

"It's all right, Miss Drew. We've got the net spread. We'll get him down, poor fellow. John, won't you come down?" he called.

I didn't know who John was. I didn't recognize Alice's voice, didn't know that that high pitch was a mark of the human female. But I knew the voice of the man. It was the man who had mocked and tortured me.

I bared my sharp little teeth and grinned defiance at him.

"Jim," I heard him say, "run back and get that pole. We'll have to poke him out of there."

"Don't hurt him! Oh, don't hurt him! Remember he's half paralyzed!" came the high-pitched voice again.

"Don't be afraid," came the response. "We'll have him down easy and comfortable."

I grinned and twittered, but the two men went on talking and paid no attention to me.

"Yes, chief," said Dean, "this is undoubtedly John Charters, who has been breaking into houses at night and frightening women half to death. I recognized him as soon as I flashed that light, despite his beard and rags. Well, once we get him back to the hospital, we'll watch him so he won't escape again. Poor fellow, I was beginning to hope he would recover. Now, after this experience—well, I don't know."

"But this bat business—it's all batty to me. How did he get the idea he was a bat?"

"Here's my explanation, chief. When the foolish fellow fired that slug into his temple, after a perfectly causeless outbreak of jealousy about me and Miss Drew—why, we've known each other since we were kids!—he blew away the whole frontal area of the brain, instantly reducing himself to the condition of an automaton, acting by purely reflex actions, like a bird or a bat. Under such conditions, his future life would be a purely vegetative one, were it not for the fact that we have two brains, one of which is never developed.

"I was trying to induce the frontal area of the right brain to take up the task laid down by the left, which had been destroyed. Had I succeeded, he would have become a human being again. I may succeed yet. He must have heard me refer to his having the brain of a bat, and, by the power of suggestion, accepted the idea that he was a bat. But this fact gives me hopes that he may yet recover."

"I think I get you, doctor. And that paralyzed arm and leg—"

"Which he spoke of as a wing? That will pass, if ever the brain resumes activity."

"And what about those descriptions of his life as a bat, that Miss Drew picked up in this place?"

"I build my strongest hopes upon those, for it is evident that poor Charters always retained a lingering doubt whether he was not a man. It is evident that the slug, which destroyed most of the frontal lobe, missed the speaking centre, and through this Charters was able to establish connection with the external world."

"I see, doctor. It's sort of beyond me, but—here comes Jim with the pole."

"Don't hurt him!" cried Alice, and ran to the base of the wall again. "John! John, darling," she cried in piteous tones, "it's Alice! You know me. Won't you come down?"

And suddenly something seemed to click in my brain. It was

as instantaneous as the click of a camera shutter. Suddenly the bat life, with all its wonder and its glory, was closed to me forever.

Suddenly I realized that I was John Charters, clinging precariously to this wall, in a vile litter of evil-smelling filth.

With three leaps I was on the ground. "Alice, I—I'm sane!" I cried. "Don't touch me!"

But her arms were around my neck, and she was sobbing out her joy upon my shoulder.

ROBERT LESLIE BELLEM

MIRROR MAGIC

His wife had given him that full-length glass,
from which his image now spoke to him! He found
himself stepping through the frame, a rejuvenated
being, prepared to play a man's part in the world!

W*ithout quite understanding* how he had become
aware of it, Marsden realized that he was suddenly not
alone in the white-tiled laboratory. Someone—or *something*—was
leaning over his shoulder as he peered intently into his microscope. A soft, feathery breath was on the nape of his neck, warm
and yet chilling.

He was vaguely annoyed. He had locked himself here in his
workroom shortly after dinner, leaving explicit instructions that
he was not to be disturbed under any circumstances. It was strange
that his wishes should be disobeyed; it had never happened before.

"Go away, please," he murmured absently.

He did not look around; because, at the moment, it was es-
sential that he keep his attention riveted upon the slide under his
microscope. For more than a year—ever since his stomach had
begun bothering him, in fact—he had been fruitlessly attempting
to isolate a certain filterable hormone, as yet undiscovered by
science and only dimly suspected of actual existence. Perhaps,
Marsden told himself as he peered into the twin eye-pieces, he
was on the verge of success with this very slide. He dared not
allow his attention to be distracted.

"Go away," he repeated.

There was no response; but the feeling persisted that he was not alone. At length it grew so strong that Marsden abandoned his attempt to dismiss it. Sighing, he raised his tired eyes from his work and looked around.

There was nobody behind him. Nobody at all.

He frowned mildly. In a vague, incurious way, he was a little startled. Purely the materialist, he held no belief in phantoms or

He heard her words through the panel: "I gave him arsenic enough to kill a dozen men."

ghosts; hence he was sure it had been no wraith whose presence he had sensed. There were no such things. *Someone had leaned over him.* Someone had breathed on his neck, with a breath at once comfortably warm yet weirdly chilling.

Now, where had that someone gone?

Marsden tried the laboratory door. It was still locked, as he had left it when he'd first entered the room this evening. The key, in fact, still reposed in the pocket of his coat, under his stained smock.

When he thought of the key, he suddenly smiled at his own bewilderment. The key. That was it. Kyra had a key, too. A duplicate key.

Kyra was Marsden's brunette wife. He'd been married to her—

was it nine years, or ten? Why, ten, of course! Ten years to the day. He felt a rueful pang when he recalled that this was their tenth anniversary. It was so stupid of him to have forgotten it. He might at least have given Kyra some little gift.

But about the key. And the breath he had felt on his neck. That must have been Kyra, he decided. She must have unlocked the door and slipped into the laboratory for an instant. Perhaps she had brought him some medicine to assuage the indigestion pains that attacked him so often of late. Seeing his preoccupation, she had probably departed as silently as she had entered. She had locked the door after her, leaving it as she'd found it.

Kyra, he mused, was more thoughtful than he had supposed her to be. Perhaps she wasn't so indifferent to him, after all. Maybe she really did consider him as more than just a mere money-making machine. He really should go and express to her his appreciation of her thoughtfulness; apologize for forgetting their anniversary. He would take her in his arms and kiss her; stroke her shoulders and glory in the soft yielding of her bosom, as he used to do in the old days, before he had become so engrossed in his work.

He left the laboratory and dragged himself wearily upstairs. His stomach was paining him again; hellishly. It was the worst attack he'd had since the trouble first started. It almost paralyzed the muscles of his legs. He clenched his teeth against a groan.

Then the agony passed. He continued his ascent. He stopped before the closed door of his wife's boudoir. "Kyra."

Yvonne, Kyra's coquettish French maid, appeared from the adjoining room. "*Madame* is asleep, *Monsieur* Marsden. It is after midnight. Do you really wish to disturb her?"

"No. Of course not." Mentally he reproached himself for his thoughtlessness. Certainly it was late. He should have realized it without being told. What could he have been thinking about? "No. Don't disturb Kyra."

The maid was staring at him oddly. "You—you seem ill, *monsieur*. You are pale. May I get you some medicine, perhaps?"

Mentally, he made a wry grimace at that. Once there had been a time when a girl like this would not have been so solicitous about his health. Instead, she might conceivably have flirted with him a bit. Yvonne looked as if she had been built for flirtations. Under her negligee, her breasts were plump and firmly rounded. Her hips possessed a sleek symmetry matched by the feminine sweep of her thighs and the dainty taper of her legs. There was a subtle aura of romantic recklessness about her....

Yes, he thought: there had been a time, perhaps ten years ago, when a girl like Yvonne might have flirted with him instead of offering him nostrums. Not that he would have responded, then or now. He had never paid any serious attention to any woman other than Kyra; nor would he.

"Medicine? No. Thank you very much, Yvonne. I'm quite all right now." Absently he started toward the stairs; then he halted. Medicine! What a wool-gathering ass he was becoming! "Medicine. That's it. That's what I came upstairs to see about. I wanted to know if Mrs. Marsden went down to my laboratory a moment ago with medicine for me. Did she, Yvonne?"

The girl seemed puzzled as she shook her head. "*Mais non, monsieur,*" she answered with unduly sharp emphasis. "*Madame* has—has not left her room since she retired."

"You are sure?"

"I am quite positive, *monsieur.*"

"Queer. Very queer. Did anyone else enter the laboratory?"

"Not to my knowledge, *monsieur.* I heard nobody. I am the only one in the house—except *madame,* of course. And yourself."

He had a strange, intuitive feeling that she was not telling the truth. But of course that was absurd. Bewildered, he shuffled back downstairs and entered his laboratory. As he closed the door and went toward his microscope, he frowned. It had been oddly real, his sensation of not being alone in this room a moment ago. Now that he was back, the remembrance was quite vivid. Yet he *had* been alone. His brain had played him a trick.

He was working too hard, he told himself. That was it. He was overtaxing his strength. Of course it had been profitable; he had made a lot of money. But he was growing old before his time.

He was only forty-one. But tonight he felt ancient... and very,

very weary. He was a tired old man who once had been rather a strapping and masculine person. His youth… that was long gone, he thought ruefully. He had squandered it.

The griping in his belly was commencing again. He could feel the pain-lines deepening in his haggard face. No wonder Kyra had so studiously avoided him recently. He was no longer buoyant and ardent, as he had been ten years ago when they were first married. He had worn himself out, making the money that kept her in luxury. But she was still young, still gay; she could still love the savor of life….

For the first time in many months, he went to the cheval mirror at the end of the room, and studied himself.

The mirror itself gave him an odd heart-twist. Kyra had bought it at an auction, soon after the honeymoon. With her own hands she had hung it in his laboratory. What was it she had said to him? Oh, yes: "I put a charm on it, darling. Whenever you look in it, you'll see the reflection of the man I love…."

He smiled. She really had loved him in those days. But that had been ten years ago. And time had wrought changes. He stared into the glass. Yes. He was old. Pain and overwork had etched their toll on his features. His hair was more grey than he had realized. His nose seemed hawk-like, bony. His cheeks were sunken—

But wait a minute! Something strange was happening to his reflection in the full-length glass. It was damnably curious. There was, suddenly, no grey in his hair. None at all. Nor could he discern any wrinkles on his face. His shoulders were no longer stooped. They were erect; almost jaunty. Almost as jaunty as the shoulders of Tommy Meade, his young assistant. What on earth was the matter with that mirror? It was distorting him; giving him a semblance that was utterly fallacious.

He stiffened as his reflected image smiled at him; *because he had not consciously smiled into the glass.* And his eyes widened stupidly *when his reflection spoke!*

It said: "I am you, John Marsden—as you were ten years ago. As you were the night you married Kyra. Don't you recognize

"Mon cher... no! You musn't go into that room!" she cried frantically.

yourself?"

It was fantastic, of course. It was completely ridiculous. Marsden had not uttered a word. And yet his own voice was ringing in his ears. Or rather, the voice that had been his when he was ten years younger!

He brushed a hand over his staring eyes. But a similar action did not take place in the mirror. "Good God!" Marsden whispered.

His reflection said: "Don't be alarmed. I'm not going to hurt you. If I'd meant to do you an injury, I could have managed it very nicely a little while ago—when I was leaning over your shoulder as you looked into that microscope."

"You—*you* were leaning over my shoulder?" Marsden choked.

"Of course." The youthful image grinned crookedly. "Ten years ago you weren't so stubbornly materialistic. Remember when Kyra said she put a charm on this mirror? You weren't as hide-bound and narrow as you are today. You might have believed in the possibility of a thing like this taking place—just as *I* believe it now. Because, after all, I am you—as you were ten years ago tonight."

Marsden felt strangely weak.

"What do you want? Why are you here?"

His image smiled at him again. "I came to exchange places with you for a few hours; to let you live again—as you used to be. You should welcome the opportunity."

Marsden said: "This is preposterous. I'm dreaming."

"Not at all," his younger self contradicted him gaily. "Step into this mirror and see for yourself. As you walk into the glass, I'll walk out. We'll trade places and identities. I'll be you; and *you* will be only a reflection. But you won't come to any harm, I assure you. Except, of course, that you'll be ten years younger. While I," the reflection added ruefully, "will be ten years older, of course."

"I'm just imagining all this," Marsden said. "But what of it? It's a curious dream, and rather pleasant." And he stepped toward the cheval glass.

There was a single instant during which he seemed to be merging himself with his mirrored image. There was another instant when he had an almost terrifying sense of duality. He was in his laboratory, and he was filled with a tingling sense of well-being; a physical completeness such as he had not known in a long time. Simultaneously, he also felt old and weary and haggard, which was normal.

Then the duality passed, and there was only the wine of youth in his veins. There was no pain in his belly. He had lost his weariness. And, curiously, all his surroundings seemed to be in reverse.

On sober thought, he could understand that. He was now in the mirror, where, obviously, everything was a reversed reflection—including himself, albeit youthfully rejuvenated. His other, pain-ridden self was in the *real* laboratory, standing before the glass.

To test this theory, he stared at the mirror. Sure enough, he saw himself as he was accustomed to being. Old; lined; stooped; toil-marked. His hands gnarled and veiny.

But when he looked down at his own hands, he saw that they were smooth and young and strong.

"God!" he whispered. "It actually happened! I'm still myself— yet I've exchanged identities with my reflection of ten years ago. *And I'm in the mirror!*" It was somewhat terrifying, especially since he had just undergone that sensation of duality, wherein he had been young, yet old; strong, yet wrinkled and grey and wracked with gut-pain.

Frightened, he moved away from the cheval glass. The instant he did so, he lost his terror; just as he lost his elderly reflection which vanished when he no longer stood before the mirror.

It was most curious. He had cast off the John Marsden whose age was forty-one. Now he was a mirrored image of that same John Marsden as of ten years ago. Erect. Not pain-torn. Not tired. Not grey. And it no longer seemed queer that his surroundings were all in reverse. Being reversed himself, everything was entirely normal to him.

He raced across the laboratory and picked up a shiny crucible of burnished chrome metal. He stared into it. Even though the reflection was distorted, he recognized his features as those of the younger John Marsden; the one who had spoken to him from the cheval glass. He was the Marsden of ten years ago, at the time of his marriage to Kyra.

Kyra! It was she who had wrought this miracle! The mirror had been her gift; she had put a charm on it. And now the charm had worked! "It's amazing!" he whispered to himself. "I must go and tell her!"

He burst from the white-walled workroom and went pelting upstairs. The surging sinews of his legs were no longer cramped. His blood sang madly in his veins as he envisioned Kyra in her boudoir; her dark eyes, her midnight hair, her glorious body that to him was the most beautiful thing in the world.

He started to knock on Kyra's door. But he was interrupted. Yvonne, the French maid, came from the adjoining room. *"Mais—* but *monsieur!"* she protested. *"Madame* is sleeping." Then, for the first time, she really looked at him.

Her amazement brought a grin to his lips. Her eyes were filled with disbelief; her crimson lips were an astounded "O" as she whispered a faint, dazed exclamation.

"What's the matter, Yvonne?" he chuckled.

"You—you have changed, *monsieur!* You are a young man! It is impossible!"

"Not at all." Of course he could not tell her what had actually taken place; she would think him a madman. Instead, he lied: "This is the way I really should look all the time—if it weren't for the pain. I just tried a new medicine. It gave me the first relief I've had in more than a year. And so—presto! I'm a new man." Once more he turned to Kyra's door and started to knock.

Yvonne surged swiftly toward him. She grabbed his wrist. *"Non, monsieur!* You must not awaken her." Her eyes looked worried.

"Why not?" He was more anxious, now, than ever, to hold Kyra in his arms; his fingers had accidentally brushed the soft curves of the French girl... he felt the warmth of her through the thinness of her negligee—and the contact sent ripples of emotion through him. He must go to Kyra! She was his wife—and he loved her! After all, it was their tenth anniversary, wasn't it?

Yvonne pressed herself against him—almost frantically, he thought. *"Madame* had a—a very severe headache when she retired. She was quite distressed; almost ill. It would be c-cruel to awaken her, *monsieur."*

A vague suspicion began to take root in the depths of his mind; but he permitted no trace of it to be revealed in his expression. Now, as the girl clung to him, he made no effort to draw away; and this time she smiled coquettishly. And he could feel the lithe softness of her body press lightly against his, as if she were drawn irresistibly to him. He wondered about that; but he thought he was beginning to understand....

Shrugging, he murmured:

"Perhaps you're right, Yvonne. I shouldn't disturb Kyra tonight. She must rest." Then, in a casual tone: "I guess I'll have a goodnight chat with Tommy Meade. He won't mind being awakened." He turned to go down the hall.

"*Mais*—but your assistant is not in," the French girl faltered. "He—went to a theater. He has not yet returned."

"Really?" Marsden's voice was dry, sardonic.

She sidled up to him again. "If *monsieur* is lonely, I—I have some fine old cognac in my own room. From France. Perhaps you would care for... some of it?"

He studied her. He noticed that in her dark eyes there slumbered, an alluring challenge; that her lips, moist and trembling a little seemed brimming with crimson allure. Through her negligee, he could see faintly the blue-veined whiteness of her arrogant young breasts, innocent of brassiere or any other concealment except the fragile gossamer of the kimono itself. And her hips were smoothly lyric; her thighs sculptured perfection. A twisted thought came to him. Why not drink with her? Why not while away an hour with her, if she'd allow it? What difference would it make?

For the first time in many months, he was beginning to see things in their true perspective. He grinned as he took Yvonne's arm. "To the cognac, my dear! And may it last... a long time!"

A single soft light glowed in her room; and there was a faint, sensual fragrance about it that stirred Marsden's newly-invigorated blood. He sprawled lazily on the chaise-longue while the French girl produced a bottle and two glasses.

They drank. And then they drank again. It was very good cognac.

Not that Marsden needed any such stimulant. His rediscovered youth was already like brandy in his veins. He felt curiously weightless, almost spritely; but there was plenty of solidity and strength in his muscles, as he proved to himself by reaching swiftly for Yvonne and pulling her down alongside him.

"*Monsieur...!*" she giggled and made a mock of pushing him

away.

His arm encircled her slim waist. "Do you like me a little, Yvonne?"

"You are... very attractive. You have an air... m-m-m! It would be difficult for any girl to be insensible to your charm, your so great fascination... *n'est-ce-pas?*"

That was pure coquetry, of course. And he thought he knew what lay behind it and caused it; just as he understood the vague hint of trouble under the liquid warmth in her eyes. In his own heart, a certain ache persisted; but he dismissed it. After all, life was very short and... love was very sweet, no matter where a man found it....

He drew Yvonne close. He kissed her full on the mouth.

She no longer struggled. Her lips parted and moved moistly, deliciously. She clasped her arms about his neck and pressed herself to him, so that he could feel the thrilling pliancy of her firm young bosom on his chest. For a moment that seemed centuries long, her mouth and his were fused together with a flux of vibrant sensation....

When at last she drew back, panting, her negligee had loosened at her throat. White breasts were subtly exposed to his avid gaze. His hands went hungrily toward her shoulders, and he fondled her with a savage tenderness that caused her to moan and whisper sharp pleasure-sounds....

"And now," he remarked with a certain touch of grimness which he could no longer filter from his voice, "I am going into *Madame's* room."

"Non, *monsieur!* Please... stay here with me!"

"I've already stayed much too long," he smiled sardonically. He walked toward the door leading into Kyra's boudoir.

Yvonne interposed herself, frantically barring his way. *"Mon cher... no!"* By a cunningly-contrived mischance she permitted the negligee to float cloudily away from her shoulders, like silken mist. The breath-taking whiteness of her figure and the gentle lilt of her bosom made him hesitate; almost caused him to forget his purpose.

Then, firmly, he thrust her aside. "You needn't try to fool me any longer, my dear. Kyra isn't in there. Is she?"

"I—I—"

He opened the door and snapped on a light. Then he grinned mirthlessly, for he had been quite correct in his guess. Kyra's bed was undisturbed. She was not in the boudoir. She had not been home since dinner-time.

Marsden turned. "Where did she go?"

"I do not know! I swear it!"

"She went out with Tommy Meade, didn't she?"

"Please, *monsieur*—you must not ask me!"

"She and Meade are together somewhere. And you were bribed to tell me that she had a headache and must not be disturbed in case I happened to inquire. Isn't that it?"

Yvonne flushed and refused to answer.

He grabbed her by the shoulders and shook her almost savagely. Her lovely breasts danced and quivered under the thin silk. "Tell me!" he demanded evenly. "Tell me, before I hurt you."

The deadliness of his voice frightened her; made her cringe. "*Oui*... you are right... *madame* is with *monsieur* Meade...."

"They're in love?"

"Y-yes."

"How long has this been going on?"

"Since he first came here to live, a y-year ago...."

That was a curious coincidence, Marsden thought. It was just about a year ago that he had begun having pains in his belly. "Where is their rendezvous? Where do they spend their time? Don't make me beat it out of you, Yvonne," he rasped.

She moaned an address, and whispered a room number.

He released her. "Thank you very much, my dear," he said slowly. "You've been quite helpful. You have opened my eyes; and you have given me much to think about... that I shall remember as long as I live. And now—good night, Yvonne."

She tried to stay him. "Wh-where are you going?"

He shook her off without answering. Hatless, he went downstairs and out to the street.

He was not conscious of walking the long blocks toward the place where Kyra and Tommy Meade kept their tryst. He was almost astonished to find himself in the lobby of the building; to hear himself renting the room next to the one where they met. He had a strange feeling of duality as he rode the elevator to the fifth floor and tipped the boy who admitted him to the chamber he had rented.

He made no light. Instead, he went quietly to the door that gave access to the adjoining room. It was locked, of course; he had expected that. But at least he could listen, with his ear pressed to the flimsy panel of thin wood.

He heard Tommy Meade's voice saying: "Hadn't we better start home now, darling?"

And Kyra's answer: "I suppose so. But, my dear, my dear, I don't want to go. Kiss me again, Tommy, sweet. Hold me… tightly. We've got an ordeal to face."

"You think he'll be done for when we get there?"

"He's *got* to be!" Kyra shrilled almost hysterically. "I put enough arsenic in his salad tonight to kill a dozen men! God—the stomach he must have! Every day I feed him a bigger dose… and still he hangs on! Damn him! *Damn him!*"

In the darkness of the next room, John Marsden recoiled. So that was it! Arsenic!

A year ago, his pains had begun. That was when Kyra and Tommy Meade had first become sweethearts; when Kyra first determined to make herself a widow. God…! A year of arsenic in daily doses! A year of gut-gripping agony! And Tommy Meade under Marsden's own roof….

…Betrayed by his assistant. Poisoned by his wife. Damned and cursed by the woman he loved—while she accepted the embraces of another man!

Slowly, like an ebbing tide, Marsden's rage abated. It was replaced by a sour, twisted mirth. How funny Kyra would look when she came home and found her schemes awry! How disconcerted she'd be to discover that her husband was a man ten years younger, virile, strong, unharmed—thanks to the magic of a mirror which she herself had given him!

It would be exquisitely humorous. He would tell her that he knew... everything. Perhaps he would even strike her in the face. Then he would order her out of the house, of course. And Tommy Meade, too. He'd laugh at them as they went. Let them starve together. Let them beg. Kyra would live in no more luxury, such as Marsden had given her. She'd end in the gutter. Good enough for her. She could go to hell.

Smiling, Marsden left the darkened hotel-room and went out into the night.

A misty rain had begun to fall. He didn't notice it. He walked toward his home. Walking seemed to calm him. He didn't mind the distance. He was lost in the seething depths of his saturnine thoughts. Once he stepped off a curb in front of a taxi; the cab careened in a wild skid on the slick asphalt as it swerved to miss him. Marsden didn't even realize how close he had come to disaster.

He kept walking.

Now he was thinking of Yvonne. Thinking of the hour he had spent in her room. In her arms. Thinking of the firm sweetness of her. The compelling ardor of her kisses. Perhaps he would allow her to remain. A man needed a woman around his home. Especially a newly-young man like himself....

Yes, he decided. Yvonne would stay.

He was nearing his house, now. It was situated on an inclined street; a bad hill in inclement weather. Without paying any attention to his movements, he started across to the opposite pavement, crossing diagonally in the middle of the block.

A truck was laboring up the slippery grade, its tire-chains clanking. And a coupe was just coming down the hill from the direction of mid-town.

Marsden saw neither vehicle. He was too preoccupied to notice.

The oncoming coupe's headlights suddenly bathed him in white glare against the night's darkness, but still he paid no heed.

(... *Within the little car, Tommy Meade yelled an oath as he wrenched his wheel. "Kyra—for God's sake—look! It's Marsden! My God—*

I'm going to hit him—I can't avoid it!"
…Kyra screamed shrilly as the coupe swerved out of control and went broadsiding down the slippery hill, on the wrong side of the street.
…The sickening skid caused the coupe to miss Marsden. But the little car crashed full into the truck which was laboring up the treacherous grade. There was a hellish din of rended metal and tinkling glass.
…Kyra's screams blended with the groans of her lover. Then the coupe burst into flames, and the screams died suddenly. There was a stench of roasted flesh…)

John Marsden was completely oblivious of the accident. He was unaware that the coupe had come close to him; that it had skidded into the heavy truck. Some external force was pulling him to his house, as if he were being drawn by a powerful psychic magnet. He gained his front door, unlocked it and entered.

He saw Yvonne racing down the stairs. She had been awakened by the sound of the crash outside. He said to her: "I want to talk to you, my dear. But I must go into my laboratory first. Something seems to be calling me in there."

Queerly, she did not answer him. She looked past him as if he had not been there; as if he had not spoken. He had an annoying sensation that she was looking *through* him, instead of staring past him.

He shrugged. She was acting as if their little hour—just a short while ago—had never been. He would talk to her about that, later. Just now his laboratory was commanding him, calling him. His ears were deaf to the licking roar of flames in the street; he had no inkling that those flames were frying the woman who had betrayed and poisoned him. He was unaware that her lover was dying beside her. He knew only that he must enter his laboratory—at once.

There was something about a mirror. Something curious. He must look at his reflection; that was it. He strode into the white-tiled room and closed the door after him. Panting, he raced to the cheval glass. "I'm here—I'm here!" he whispered.

His mirrored image was that of an old, pain-haggard man. That was ridiculous; he didn't look like that at all. But wait—! The reflection was changing. It became younger, more erect, more jaunty.

...As it changed, John Marsden felt a weariness creeping into his bones; felt the flesh sluffing away from his sunken cheeks. He doubled over as a knife-sharp pain tore into his belly like a bayonet.

He was passing through the mirror, into his laboratory. His *real* laboratory, not its reflection. He suddenly wanted to vomit. His stomach was full of white-hot irons of agony. "Yvonne— Yvonne—!" he cried out.

Then there was no John Marsden in the mirror. There was no John Marsden in the laboratory. There was only John Marsden's corpse. That was what Yvonne found when she raced into the room in response to his call.

Her eyes widened, *"Le pauvre vieux!* The poor old man!" she whispered. "Here he has been dying in this room all evening, while I lay upstairs asleep; while I might have been with him, helping him!"

The coroner called it murder by arsenic poisoning. But of course neither Kyra nor Tommy Meade could be prosecuted for the crime. They were dead.

By a grim coincidence, they had lost their lives in an automobile accident. As nearly as could be determined, they had died at the exact moment of John Marsden's own passing.

REX NORMAN

DANCE OF DAMBALLA

*Man turns into serpent and a girl loses her
soul to the god in the weird voodoo rites
that the magician has brought to Harlem!
Only Derek's Thunderstone Ouanga can
save her from complete dishonor*

Marius the Magician bowed politely to the applause
and then prepared to do his last trick. The night club
patrons at the nearest tables hitched their chairs closer to the
dance floor that served as his stage. Those further away stood up
to get a better view of the tall, lean faced man who stood in the
spotlight's glare. The whispering died down as Marius waited for
silence.

"I see many familiar faces here tonight," he said. "That means
that many of you have seen this next trick before." He picked up
a birdcage with a dove in it and held it up for all to see. "For you
others who have never seen it, I will explain that it is a variation
of the great Houdini's bird cage trick. I shall count three slowly
and then the bird cage will disappear under your very eyes, leaving
only the bird." He smiled quietly around at the intent faces.
"Watch closely. If you are very quick, perhaps you will be able to
tell how it is done. Ready?"

"Shoot!" answered a voice from somewhere in the darkness and
again Marius smiled. He held the cage in his two hands close to
his chest and those at the nearest tables could see the dove preen-
ing its feathers and blinking its quick eyes as if it were winking.

Then,

"One!" said Marius. "Two… and three!" His two hands clapped together with a loud smack and both the cage and the bird were gone!

He continued to stand there for the space of a heart beat, unmoving, and then, as the hushed audience held its breath, down from the darkness above his head fluttered the dove. It circled him for a moment, then settled on his outstretched forefinger and again started to preen its feathers as the storm of applause filled the room.

Marius bowed again and again to the thunderous clapping, then the spotlight went out and he slipped from the center of the floor to the table in the corner where Erica and her younger brother, Derek, sat.

"I still think you're tops, Marius," said Derek. "I've seen you do that trick about fifty times and it still has me fooled. Do you use…?"

"You know Marius won't tell you, Derek," said Erica in her warm throaty voice. "Why do you keep on asking?" and as she spoke she took Marius' hand and pulled him down to the cushioned bench beside her.

"For the same reason he keeps on asking you to marry him," answered Derek through the darkness. "We can't help it, either of us."

Marius chuckled and slipped an arm around Erica's lovely body. It was warm, soft and fragrant under the sheer silk of her evening dress and it yielded to the pressure of his hand, moving closer to him. Then he sensed rather than saw her turn up her face to him and he pressed a burning, searching kiss on her mouth. Her bare arms stole up around his neck, her firm, rounded breasts crushed themselves against his chest, and he felt a delicious tremor run through her lithe dancer's body as his grip tightened.

"Say, what's going on there?" asked Derek. "Seems to me the temperature's rising." Erica's arms fell away from Marius' neck and she sat back with a light laugh.

"We were just deciding to go home," said Marius. "How about it?"

"Home?" repeated Derek. "Why, the floor show isn't even over yet! And the next number's the one I wanted to see most, the Voodoo Dancers!"

"We'll wait," Erica reassured him. "The evening's young yet." And she squeezed Marius' hand as if in promise.

The spot light went on again but now there was a blue-green slide in front of it and it cast a dim and eerie light on the dance floor. Strange, exotic shrubs and plants had been placed before the orchestra platform while the room was darkened and against this tropical background stood the squat figure of Joe Monelli, owner of the Qub Haytien. He raised a pudgy hand for silence.

"And now, ladies and gentlemen," he announced. "The high spot of our evening's entertainment... and the high spot of *all* New York's night life! The act I had hoped to be able to get when

I opened the Club Haytien, but one which it was impossible to arrange for until tonight! The real, the authentic Voodoo dancers from Hayti! Brought here from that island of mystery at great expense!"

As a buzz of excited talk broke out he raised his hand again and then turned to the table where Marius, Erica, and Derek sat.

"As it happens, we have someone here tonight who knows a

Eyes aflame, he slithered after her while she shivered in apparent ecstasy.

good deal about Voodoo. Marius the Magician lived in Hayti for many years, and I'm going to let him tell you something about the dances we are about to witness." With a sly smile, he bowed to Marius and left the floor.

A faint frown of annoyance furrowed Marius' brow as he rose slowly to his feet. This was something he was completely unprepared for. So that was why Monelli had asked him what he knew about Hayti, about Voodoo; and that was why the club's owner had refused to tell him anything about the new act he had booked to follow him, Marius. He had not wanted to prepare him, feeling that an extemporaneous description of the dances would be more effective and seem more real in an intimate club.

Then Marius' face cleared. He was enough of a showman to be able to carry it off. Let them bring on their Harlem negroes in a fake Voodoo dance and he would try and make it seem authentic.

"I don't expect any of you to believe me," he said to the attentive guests. "But I had no idea I was to be called on to act as master of ceremonies. I don't even know what dances our next performers are planning to do, but with your permission, I'll ask them when they get on the floor."

Then the spotlight went out and there was darkness again. It seemed thicker, more palpable than before and somehow the air had become heavier, harder to breathe, filled with an electric tension.

Marius felt beads of perspiration come to his brow for the temperature had somehow risen to an almost tropical degree. Then there came the soft rattling of a drum, like a signal, and the spot went on again. There, standing against the background of the tropical plants, were four dark skinned figures.

In the center were a man and a woman. The man was huge, burly, with a shaven, apelike head and narrow, slit eyes. He was wearing a white loin cloth but nothing more. The woman was young, slim. Her high, erect breasts were covered by a gay bandanna like the one she wore turban fashion on her head. A grass skirt circled her middle but her bronze legs were bare. To the right of the man was a drummer crouching over his big, skin-covered drum. To the left of the woman stood a lean, wizened old man. He wore a white surplice embroidered with feathers over his shoulders and a red turban was wound around his head.

Marius looked at the four negroes and those near him saw him start, his eyes widen. Then he snapped a quick question at the old man in the half French jargon spoken by the blacks in Hayti and everyone listened intently as the old man answered. He spoke for several seconds and then stopped. There was a strange look in Marius' eyes as he turned to the waiting guests.

"This is something I would never have believed possible," he said. "I expected that our friends here might do the *Danse Congo*, a wild native dance. But instead they tell me that they are going to do the *Danse Damballa*, a dance of their *Service Petro* or Voodoo Rites!"

He looked around the hushed night club. "You probably think this is part of an act, but I tell you that I lived in Hayti for ten years and only once, with great difficulty, managed to see this dance! Ti Mich'," he nodded to the old man, "is a *papaloi* or high priest of the *Service Petro* and he won't tell me why they came to this country to do this dance. He will only say that they got permission from Damballa Oueddo, their god. That man," he pointed to the burly buck who stood next to the girl, "is carrying the *Rada* bells."

As if he understood, the negro held out the short iron bar with the bells on it for all to see, then rested it on his shoulder again. "The bar and bells are forged out of iron slave collars and chains and its very possession is punishable by imprisonment in Hayti… for before it can be used in the *Danse Damballa*, it must be smeared with the brains of a *blanc* or white man!"

A gasp went through the intent audience and Derek, leaning close to Erica, whispered, "What a showman!"

"And now," went on Marius, "the *Danse Damballa!* The dance of the serpent god, Damballa Oueddo and his wife, Ayida Oueddo! Please let me warn you not to try and leave during the dance or to do anything that might disturb the dancers. If you do, I cannot answer for the consequences!" He sat down.

There was a moment of hushed silence, then Ti Mich', the *papaloi* raised two bleached thigh bones high above his head, beat them together and the dance started. First there was only the drum beaten by the heels of the drummer's hands, then rubbed with a rosined thumb so that it roared like a raging bull. Then the clicking rattle of the bones in the *papaloi's* hands joined it and finally the soft, eerie tinkle of the *Rada* bells, a delicate but insistent sound that cut through the rhythm of the drum like the blade of a machete.

With an agile leap, the big black leaped into the center of the dance floor. He landed in a half crouch and whirled the *Rada* bells over his head in a humming circle. Then he began the invocation to Ayida Oueddo, the Mother Goddess, imploring her to appear. He postured, spun and uttered harsh, guttural cries, bounding higher and higher, whirling the *Rada* bells faster and faster until finally, his body gleaming with sweat, he fell prostrate to the floor.

Now the drum became softer, slower, its beat more insistent, and into the eerie glow of the spotlight glided the woman. Her body was young but ageless. She seemed taller than she had before and incredibly lovely. She was a woman no longer but the goddess Ayida Oueddo. In her hands she carried a cup filled with Three Thieves Water, and she placed this on her head. Then, her hands on her hips, she went into the dance of transformation, changing the man who groveled before her on the ground into a snake.

Round and round him she spun, her eyes glittering, her erect breasts rising and falling, the muscles on her bared stomach quivering, but with a fixed expression on her face. Shudders shook her body, twisted the smooth flesh of her thighs as she whirled and swayed faster and faster. Then, taking the cup of Three Thieves Water from her head, she took a mouthful and spat it on the prostrate man. He screamed once as if seared by living flame, then he started to change into Damballa Oueddo, the Serpent.

Each limb seemed to writhe and twist separately. His body seemed to become jointless and as the drum thudded louder and louder, he slithered over the floor like an ape-headed snake after the fleeing woman. Louder and louder beat the drum until its volume was almost unbearable. Nearer and nearer drew the writhing black to the erect girl, then with a quick movement he had seized her, not with his hands, but seemingly by twisting his body around her like the very snake he represented. The drums stopped. The woman screamed once, then the spotlight went out and there was only darkness and the silence of a hundred held breaths.

When the house lights went on, the floor was empty but the patrons still sat silent under the spell of that ancient, compelling and evil dance. The drink-flushed faces of the men had become pale. The jaded eyes of hard-faced divorcees, glittering. The bold sensuality of what they had witnessed had affected them all. Then, as the thunderous applause broke out, Marius, his jaw set, rose to his feet and led Erica and Derek from the room.

Marius stopped removing the grease paint from his face and looked at Erica in his dressing room mirror.

"I don't expect you to understand," he said. "But I tell you that Monelli is playing with fire! That's not a dance they did tonight, it's an actual rite in the *Service Petro!* God knows what it will lead to if he permits them to go on again here!"

"That's ridiculous!" said Erica. "It was the most exciting, thrilling performance I've ever seen and it gave me just the idea I've been looking for!"

Marius' eyes widened. "You don't mean…?"

"Exactly! Mercer wanted me to work out a completely new type of dance for the second act finale of his revue. Something sensational, startling. This is the dance!"

Marius continued to look at her for a moment, then he grinned sardonically.

"And you think you can dance it just after having seen it once?" he asked. "You think that the motions, the steps and the music are all there are to it? I tell you that no one can dance it who doesn't *believe* in Damballa and Ayida! Believe in the final metamorphosis from man into snake… and love the snake!"

Erica stared at him angrily.

"Listen, save that for part of your act! Just because you're a professional magician you think that you have to shroud every-

She was lying there quietly when he got back, and though her face was pale, her breathing was regular.

thing in mystery!"

"Please, Erica…" began Marius, but she interrupted him impatiently.

"I'm going to do that dance in Mercer's new revue!" she said. "And I'm not going to learn it just by watching! I'm going to have it *taught* to me!" And then she had opened the dressing room door and was gone.

Derek started to go after her but Marius stopped him with a motion of his head.

"Let her be," he said. "First of all she won't be able to make Ti Mich' understand what she wants. And then, even if he does understand, he'll only laugh at her."

Derek's face was troubled.

"I don't like it," he muttered. "It was one thing to watch that dance, but to think of Erica doing it...."

"Forget it," said Marius. "She hasn't got a chance in the world of ever really doing it." He went back to removing his make-up.

When Marius and Derek left the dressing room, Erica wasn't in the corridor outside. They looked in the adjoining rooms, thinking that she might be visiting one of the other performers, but none of them had seen her. Then when they went to the club's door to see if she were waiting outside for them, John, the doorman, told them.

"Sure!" he said. "I put her in a cab with those four Voodoo dancers just a few minutes ago."

Marius, his face suddenly pale, seized Derek by the arm.

"Quick! Get your car! I'll be right back!" and turning, he ran into the night club like a madman. He found Monelli at the bar.

"Those Voodoo dancers!" he snapped. "Where are they staying?"

Monelli gaped at him, frightened by his urgency.

"Let's see. Somewhere in Harlem." His eyes blinked as he tried to collect himself, then he remembered the address and told it to Marius. Without a word of explanation Marius dashed out of the bar and down the corridor to his dressing room. He started hunting frantically through his open trunks for something and he finally found it in the bottom of a battered kit bag, then he ran out of the dressing room and got to the club's door just as Derek pulled up at the wheel of his car. Marius leaped in, the motor roared and then they were off, swinging round the corner on two wheels.

Though Derek glanced again and again at Marius' set face during the wild ride up to Harlem, it was almost a half hour later before the magician spoke.

He glanced at a street sign as they whizzed past it, then said, "This is the block. Stop here."

Derek slammed on the brakes and pulled up to the curb. Marius was out of the car almost before it had stopped rolling. Derek started to get out also, but Marius checked him.

"No!" he said. "Stay here and wait! And keep your motor running!"

Derek started to protest, but something in Marius' eye silenced him and he sat back. Then Marius was running silently up the dark and deserted street looking for the house number that Monelli had given him.

It was the third house from the corner and there was a dark alley beside it. He stopped in front of it for just a moment, listening, then he heard what he had expected, yet feared to hear; the soft, gradually quickening thudding of a tom-tom. He cursed softly under his breath, then he was moving like a ghost down the alley.

The alley was pitch dark except for one shaft of light that knifed through a crack in a closed wooden shutter and it was to that crack that he glued his eye. He was looking into a dingy tenement room, yet what was taking place inside of it was ancient before the first white man set foot in America.

There were four negroes who had done the Voodoo dance at the Club Haytien, only now the woman was not standing up with the other three but squatting in the corner against the wall. In her place, her bare white arms in vivid contrast with the gleaming black bodies, stood Erica!

Her eyes were wide, intent, as she watched the big black leap into the center of the floor, the *Rada* bells swinging over his head. Louder thudded the drum, faster clicked the thigh bones in the *papaloi's* hand, faster and faster whirled and spun the Haitian in the wooing dance, begging Ayida to come to him.

Then came Erica's cue; placing the cup of Three Thieves Water on her head, she glided out to join him. Her head rigid to balance the cup, her body writhed and swayed sinuously. Her hips twisted and her firm, unfettered breasts danced tremulously under the clinging fabric of her evening dress. It was beautiful, exciting, seductive, but it was not the Dance of Damballa. The postures, the contortions of her lithe body were the same as those of the girl who had performed at the club, but there was something missing.

"'*Rettez!* Stop!" commanded Ti Mich'. The drumming stopped. Erica turned wondering eyes toward him, and he shook his head slowly. From a pouch at his waist he took a pinch of ochre and before Marius could do more than clench his fists involuntarily, the *papaloi* had marked her forehead with it. Marked her as Damballa's own with his zigzag snakey sign!

Erica flinched as if his touch had burned her; then she shivered and her eyes took on the burning, unholy light that had been in the negress's eyes when she had danced. Ti Mich' seized the neck of her evening dress and ripped it from her, and she stood there clad only in a tight fitting bandeau with a sheer wisp of silk around her middle, yet completely unaffected by her half nudity.

Again the thigh bones clicked. Again the booming roar of the drum began and again Erica danced. But now she was changed: now she was Ayida Oueddo! Her bare white limbs shivered and pulsed with apparent ecstasy. Her hips swayed with pagan abandon as the Haitian writhed nearer and nearer her on the floor.

Marius was spellbound, the blood hammering in his temples, completely forgetful of what he had come to do. For Erica had taken the Three Thieves Water in her mouth and spat it on the man at her feet. Now he was no longer a man but Damballa, the Snake God, slithering after her with eyes aflame. Faster and faster whirled Erica, eluding yet enticing, her breasts straining to escape the covering of the confining silk.

Finally as if coming out of a trance Marius snapped into action.

He took the object he had hunted in his dressing room from his pocket. It was a skin bag with a thong fastened to it. He slipped the thong over his head and around his neck, then seizing the edge of the shutter, he ripped it away from the window. The drummer, the *papaloi* and the negress swung around as he leaped into the room, but Erica, and the writhing man on the floor, entranced by the fever of their dance, only drew closer together. Now he drew back like a snake striking and lunged forward to wrap his gleaming body about hers; but even as he moved, Marius leaped forward and stamped down on his bull neck just as he would have done to crush the head of a venomous snake.

The snake dancer screamed once, then lay still, writhing feebly. But now, with a shriek of outrage, the *papaloi* drew himself up to his full height. Pointing a skinny forefinger at Marius, he fixed him with his reptilian eyes. Marius felt his flesh creep as if a loathsome worm were crawling over his body. Ti Mich's finger was making the zigzag sign of Damballa and now in a hissing voice he was laying his curse on him.

"Strike with thy poison fangs, Oh, Damballa! Shrivel the flesh from his bones! Seethe his eyes in the sockets of his skull! Boil him...."

"Stop!" Marius' voice cracked like a whip. "Stop, lest I turn your curse back on you!" and his face pale but set, he lifted the skin bag he had put around his neck and held it out for the *papaloi* to see. The aged negro's eyes widened.

"A Thunderstone *Ouanga!*"

"Yes, a *ouanga* given me by Ti Tepi, the greatest Two Headed Doctor in all Hayti! It can turn your *obeah* as the Thunderstone turns the blade of a knife!"

The face of Ti Mich' was twitching with baffled rage, then suddenly it became expressionless again and an unholy light flickered in the depths of his beady eyes.

"You want her?" he pointed to the dull eyed and shuddering Erica. "Then take her and go!" Marius swung the half nude dancer's body up in his arms, the *papaloi* started to laugh. He laughed louder and louder as Marius hurried across the room carrying Erica, then as he swung her out of the window and followed her, the laughter was swelled by that of the drummer, the girl, and the man who still groveled on the floor... and that was the last thing that Marius heard as he carried Erica down the alley to the car, peal on peal of mocking, soul-shaking, dark laughter!

The ride to Erica's house was like a journey in a dream. She sat between Marius and Derek unmoving, unwinking, uttering no sound even when they spoke to her. It was as if she had left something behind in that dingy room where she had tried to learn the Dance of Damballa; as if her brother and the man who loved her were carrying away only her shell. Then, when the car stopped, she swayed forward and would have fallen if it had not been for Marius' encircling arm. Curses were rising in his throat but they never came from his lips, for a fear that was almost madness had sealed his lips.

Everything was hushed when Derek opened the apartment door and Marius carried her in and put her on the couch. It was as if an invisible wall isolated them from the rest of the world. No street noises came to their ears. The only sound was Erica's stertorous breathing as she lay on the couch with closed eyes.

Derek kept glancing nervously at Marius, his face pale.

"Is she unconscious? Shall I call a doctor?"

Marius' jaw muscles twitched. "You won't find the kind of doctor she needs in New York," he answered. "The only kind that could help her would be a Two Headed Doctor! A witch doctor!"

"But Good God! It's impossible! Incredible! Isn't there something I...."

"Not you. There's nothing you can do. And I... I can only prepare." Marius, his face mask-like, took the skin pouch from around his neck. He opened it and fumbled with its contents, then he found what he wanted and took it out. It lay in his palm for a minute and Derek could see that it was a bullet, but a bullet that gleamed in the moonlight. A silver bullet.

Then Marius took a revolver from his hip pocket, removed the cartridges it contained and loaded it with the single silver bullet. Then he put the gun back in his pocket and fixed his eyes on Erica.

They were not the eyes of a man looking on the half nude body of the woman he loves, admiring the heaving orbs of her breasts, the swelling curves of her hips, the shapely taper of her lovely limbs. They were the eyes of an avenger waiting for the appearance of an enemy and they seemed to be boring into her brain as if tracing to its source the spell that held her. Then her breathing became louder; suddenly her eyes opened and she smiled... but it was a smile that made Marius' blood run cold! The slow, unholy smile of a woman welcoming a demon lover!

Before either Marius or Derek could move she was off the couch and standing in the center of the half dark room, a lithe figure of savage loveliness incarnate. She stood there a moment, poised, listening; then as if at a signal from some eerie music that their ears could not hear, she started to dance again! She started to writhe in the slow, sinuous motions of the Dance of Damballa!

Derek's face was ashen, his eyes dilated. Marius was sitting as if spellbound while, eyes closed, the possessed woman whirled faster and faster in the role of Ayida Oueddo. Her hips swayed; her limbs trembled frenziedly. Her breasts rose and fell faster and faster. Her slim legs flashed and her back arched. Wilder and wilder became her movements as she reached the climax of the dance. Now she was moving backward as if luring on the invisible Damballa. Her eyes rolled upward in ecstasy her mouth half open. Suddenly she froze, her eyes opened wide with terror, and she shrieked like a lost soul!

It was as if she had suddenly awakened from a hellish dream; as if she had suddenly become herself... and found that self in the grip of a loathesome and horrible serpent!

She stood there, completely alone in the center of the half dark room, yet they could see her muscles contracting, her hands moving feebly as if invisible coils were looped around her. They stared transfixed as she fell writhing and twisting to the floor, plucking at thin air. Was it the contortions of her own body that made her breasts seem to flatten out as if by the crushing of some invisible force? Did they imagine the dark red weals as of some constricting agent that appeared on her snowy thighs?

With a snarl Marius leaped to his feet and ran like a madman out of the door. He heard Derek shouting hysterically after him, but he knew what he had to do. The car was still at the door and he leaped into it and was snapping on the ignition even as he slammed the door. He went roaring through the dark streets to

The last thing Marius heard was peal on peal of mocking, soul-shaking, dark laughter!

the sound of screaming tires so fast that the red lights he passed were like winking eyes.

The snarl was still on his lips when he reached the garbage littered street that he had left but a short time before. Brakes squealing, he slammed the car against the curb at the mouth of the dark alley and then he was pounding down it to where a square of light came through the shattered window. He put his hands on the sill to leap inside, then his glance went through the opening to the dingy room and a low moan of horror came from his lips, his legs started to buckle underneath him and it was only his grip on the window ledge that kept him from falling.

There had been four blacks in the room when he left it. Now it was empty… of humans! A packing case draped with a feather decorated cloth stood against the far wall like an altar now. On it six candles burned in the double triangle or pentacle, and in the center of the pentacle was the most terrible and horrifying thing he had ever dreamed of; a wax image that even at this distance he could see was the image of Erica and wrapped around it, crushing it slowly and inexorably to a shapeless mass was a small, brightly banded snake!

For the space of a heart beat he could not move, the paralysis of his horror holding him spellbound. The triangular head of the reptile was swaying from side to side, its forked tongue flickering as it gripped the waxen image tighter and tighter in its loathesome coils. Then with a hoarse yell, Marius had leaped through the window and into that hellish room. The snake's beady eyes were on him now and they seemed quick with unholy intelligence. Marius whipped the gun from his pocket and steadying his trembling hand, fired… once!

The snake's headless body continued to writhe for just an instant, then slowly the quivering coils unwrapped themselves, loop after loop, hung on the edge of the packing case for an instant, then dropped with a soft thud to the floor.

Marius looked down at the still twitching body then up at the rickety door in the wall behind the packing case. Gritting his teeth he forced himself to walk towards it. He opened it and looked inside, then he shut it again and went back towards the window and his face was white and sick, a mingling of horror and disbelief.

Erica was lying on the couch again when he got back to her apartment. Her face was pale but her breathing was regular. When he knelt beside her, her eyes opened and she smiled, lifting her head slightly for his kiss. She sighed like a tired child and taking his hand, she closed her eyes and went to sleep.

Derek sat in a chair as if in a daze. Even when Marius told him what he had seen in the center of the pentacle on the crude altar, no light of understanding came to his eyes.

"It's… it's all just a nightmare," he said finally. "None of it really happened. We'll wake up soon and find we dreamed it all."

Slowly Marius shook his head.

"No," he said. "It did happen. How or why, only God knows. But suppose, just suppose that Damballa Oueddo had tired of dark skinned women. Suppose he wanted a white woman. Suppose that was why he let his priest come to New York and perform the sacred dance here. Suppose…."

"Stop it! Stop it!" moaned Derek. "I don't want to hear any more! There's some rational explanation for it all, I tell you!"

"There is? What about what I found in the room behind the altar after I shot the snake? Ti Mich', the *papaloi,* lying on the floor with a bullet hole in his head?"

"You used a silver bullet. It has greater penetrating power than a lead one. It went through the door and killed him!"

Marius merely looked strangely at him. Why tell him that there was no hole in the door? That the bullet could not have gone through it… *because he had seen the flattened slug lying on the floor just behind the altar!*

82499490R00111

Made in the USA
Columbia, SC
17 December 2017